W9-BDZ-948

THESE ARE UNCORRECTED ADVANCE PROOFS
BOUND FOR YOUR REVIEWING CONVENIENCE

In quoting from this book for reviews or any other purpose, it is essential that the final printed book be referred to, since the author may make changes on these proofs before the book goes to press.

An allusive psychological mystery filled with murders, corruption, politics Southern-style, and shadowy conspiracies.

"In *Sacrament of Lies*, the line between certainty and madness is as thin as a razor and equally as dangerous. Elizabeth Dewberry has given us a rare gift, a literary thriller that will keep us up all night. This book is riveting. " —Ann Patchett

---

When Grayson Guillory begins to suspect her power-hungry father, the governor of Louisiana, and her new husband of murdering her mother, she finds herself questioning her own sanity. She knows her mother suffered from manic depression and believes she committed suicide. But then Grayson discovers a video in which her mother accuses the governor of plotting her murder, and those bitter accusations strike a chord.

Is it murder or suicide? As she searches for clues to help divine the truth, Grayson both fears that she has inherited her mother's delusional illness, and fears that she hasn't. In this world of ghosts and ambiguous facts, no evidence seems final. Grayson is torn between loyalty to the memory of the mother she loved and loyalty to her father, whose charismatic ambition at once attracts and repels her. To make matters worse, her father has hastily married her mother's younger sister, Audrey. And while her father's marriage seems happy, Grayson's own new marriage is faltering under the weight of her suspicions.

Written in a fluid and captivating dramatic monologue that leads to a stunning showdown, Elizabeth Dewberry's atmospheric story explores how some families nurture cruel secrets at the expense of truth and redefine love in attempts to accommodate evil. *Sacrament of Lies* raises questions about family, love, loyalty, ambition, and morality in a kind of modern-day Hamlet set in New Orleans with the genders reversed.

ELIZABETH DEWBERRY is the author of two previous novels, *Many Things Have Happened Since He Died* and *Break the Heart of Me*. She lives in the Florida panhandle.

Online excerpt available at www.penguinputnam.com/excerpts

SACRAMENT OF LIES

SACRAMENT OF LIES

Elizabeth Dewberry

BlueHen Books

a member of Penguin Putnam Inc. New York 2002

BlueHen Books
a member of
Penguin Putnam Inc.
375 Hudson Street
New York, NY 10014

Library of Congress Cataloging-in-Publication Data

Dewberry, Elizabeth.
Sacrament of lies / by Elizabeth Dewberry.
p.   cm.
ISBN 0-399-14854-X
1. Children of governors—Fiction.   2. Fathers and daughters—Fiction.   3. Mothers—Death—Fiction.   4. Married women—Fiction.
5. Louisiana—Fiction.   I. Title.
PS3572.A936S24   2002   2001037716
813'.54—dc21

Printed in the United States of America

1   3   5   7   9   10   8   6   4   2

This book is printed on acid-free paper.

BOOK DESIGN BY AMANDA DEWEY

I'm very grateful to be publishing this book with the people at BlueHen Books, who care deeply about literary fiction and are committed to publishing it well. I particularly want to thank my editor, Greg Michalson, for his musical ear, gentle spirit, and keen intelligence.

For

Robert Olen Butler,

my husband and best friend

SACRAMENT OF LIES

I T'S THE LAST AFTERNOON OF MARDI GRAS, and I sit here, very still, on the steps outside St. Louis Cathedral, looking out over Jackson Square, and wait. I look in the eyes of drag queens and beer vendors and jokers with knives in their heads, study the faces of tarot card readers and topless tourists and housewives in masks made of feathers.

Somebody's trying to kill me. Or at least lock me up.

It's also possible I'm being paranoid. I still don't completely trust myself—I haven't been threatened, I have no hard evidence—but I trust my father even less.

This much I do know: My father, the Governor of Louisiana, killed my mother. He had at least two people's help, not counting mine, both of whom are dead. I didn't know I was involved. I destroyed the evidence, which, at the time and for what it's worth, I thought was proof she'd killed herself. But now I know what happened—or not everything, but enough, more than I wish I knew—and I'm the only person left, besides my father, who does. So who's to say he won't kill me?

He couldn't do it himself. I still believe that. But I no longer feel certain he wouldn't hire someone.

Take care of Grayson, he would say. *Take care.*

Though I can't imagine who he'd say it to. The circle around my father is smaller than ever, tightening, like a noose, and I won't know the man—it will be a man—but I won't know who until he pulls a gun or a knife or offers me a drink that turns out to be poison.

So I'm trying to come up with a defense.

There's a cop nearby, a cop on a horse, and I'm afraid of horses, but I could get over that if I thought he'd save my life. I'm not going to trust the police, though. I can't trust anybody.

My mother's pistol sits in my purse, tight as the knot in my stomach, but I'm not going to pull it out here, in the crowd.

All I've got, then, is I'm safest where I am, out in the open, surrounded by strangers.

Everything's happening very slowly, in vivid detail, as if I've already been shot through the heart and my brain is trying to stretch out my last moments in this life. A Dixieland jazz band and a guitar-strumming gospel singer and a ragged group of senior citizens with saws and spoons and a washboard for instruments are all making music at once, but I hear each note separately, one after the other, the way seconds move through time, and I feel a clock running down in my chest, gravity pulling at my throat.

An angry young woman with a crown of thorns tattooed on her forehead yells into a bullhorn, describing a lake of fire as if she's drunk from it, swum through it, bathed in it. A man in a turban draws a kerosene circle around himself and lights it with a match. He picks up a handful of flames and puts it in his mouth, rolls it on his tongue as if it's a delicacy in his home country.

I can almost taste it with him. I feel the heat in my mouth and taste something bitter, like ashes.

As the circle burns itself out, I'm smelling warm beer and sunburned skin and something sweet and earthy and full of yearning, like pipe smoke from a distance, or pot. Mostly, though, I watch the flow of people, hoping somehow I'll know the man I'm waiting for when he comes.

A monk in a purple robe carrying a dead frog on a cross moves toward me, and I stand up, ready for anything, but he doesn't have a gun. He has a leather whip for a belt, though. If he wants me to come with him, I'll start screaming—I won't go—and I take a big breath so I'll be able to yell, but he hands me an orange card that says, "Get Out of Purgatory Free."

"Trust in frogs," he says to me, and then, louder, to the preacher, "Praise frogs."

He moves away, and I turn the card over, but the other side is blank.

The tattooed preacher ignores him.

I turn around, my back exposed to the crowd, to go into the Cathedral. I'm not Catholic—I'm not even particularly religious—but I feel like praying, and I can't do it out here. I want a man who believes what he's saying to tell me, "This is what's true." I want him to lay his hands on me, healing. I want to be promised life and told to go in peace.

The church is locked, though, and empty. It's Shrove Tuesday, which the faithful supposedly spend in penance, preparing for Ash Wednesday, and a sign on the door says next confession is in an hour. It's open all day tomorrow, which does me no good today.

I sit back down on the stairs and look at the monk's card, sweat-stained now, in my hand.

It's hot, and I'm thirsty.

I don't believe in purgatory, but if I'm wrong and it's real, my mother's been there for the past year. My husband, Carter, and my mother's former lover, Dr. Fontenot, have been there less than a week, assuming they didn't go straight to hell.

I get my lighter out of my pocket—I've started smoking again— and set the card on fire and light a cigarette off the flame and let the card drop onto a stone stair. Then I watch the words on the paper crumble into ashes, and I crush out the embers with my foot.

I pull smoke from the cigarette deep into my lungs, fill myself with it.

I'm half-expecting my father to show up, just appear out of the crowd and walk over to me and sit down. I left a message on his private machine saying I'd be here, asked him to meet me, though who knows if he'll come. Crowds like this are always a security risk, which won't stop him unless he wants it to.

I've decided to tell him everything. I have nothing to lose now. *I know what you did*, I will say to him. *I know that you killed her*. Then I'll see what he does.

I‍T STARTED WITH A BOOK, A HARDCOVER copy of T. Harry Williams's massive biography of our most powerful, most hated, arguably most loved, and only assassinated governor, Huey Long. I hadn't read it, didn't remember buying it, but I was packing my things to move in with Carter when I found it on my shelf. I picked it up—it wasn't heavy enough for a book its size—and it fell open, and the first few pages were regular pages, but the rest had been glued together and hollowed out with a razor blade or X-Acto knife, and there was a videotape inside, an unmarked video.

This is not my book, not my video.

I closed the book and put it in the box.

My first thought was, *How do I know with absolute certainty that I've never been videotaped having sex?*

I moved on to travel. Bali, Turkey, Finland, New Zealand, all trips my ex-husband and I planned but never took, all went in the box.

But then again, how could I not know?

Which wasn't as much of a comfort as it might have been if it hadn't led directly to this: *But chances are, my father has.*

My father's womanizing was a loudly whispered secret in Louisiana, one I was not at all interested in knowing any more about than I did.

I packed Eastern religion and *How to Discover Your Past Lives*, a phase I went through after my divorce, before I decided I had enough on my mind without borrowing dead people's problems.

I should just throw it in the trash and try to forget about it.

Which is something like being handed a subpoena and tearing it up without reading it—whatever was there, it's not going away, and having gotten rid of it for the moment doesn't keep you from obsessing over every past indiscretion, every enemy you might ever have made, every possible mess you could find yourself involved in, not to mention a few impossible ones. If anything, it just makes things worse.

So I left it in the box to wait until I could watch it alone. I would have watched it then and there, but we'd been gradually moving in together since my mother died, and my VCR was already at Carter's.

I packed my mysteries next, which were all the same size, which was a comfort. My mother had died three months earlier, and I was still waking up from the same dream almost every night, afraid to go back to sleep and afraid to stay awake. So I'd read crime novels until morning—plucky, never-married female detectives who kept sticking their noses where they didn't belong until they found themselves alone in a bar with a guilt-stricken murderer who was ready to confess. They had their appeal: all the questions got answered, all the bad guys got what they deserved, nobody got away with anything.

I took a lettuce crate into the kitchen and set it on the counter to do my crystal, and while I stood there wadding up newspaper to line the crate, trying not to read the news—I was stressed out enough already—I started getting nervous.

I don't know where that video came from or when or how it got here or why whoever's trying to tell me something doesn't just pick up the phone and call—I'm not listed, but if they can get in my apartment, they could find my number—so whatever's going on here, it's not good.

I grabbed a plastic Mardi Gras cup out of the cabinet, filled it with tap water, and drank it slowly. It tasted like chlorine, which was reassuring—the germs were probably dead. The month before, two hundred people in Baton Rouge had gotten sick from bacteria in the water, though Carter had kept it out of the news. I threw the cup away.

My chest hurt, my body telling me I was too wound up.

Inhale.

My mother was always fighting her fears with medication, which didn't ultimately work, so I'd been trying to switch my stress-management techniques over to deep breathing and chamomile tea.

Exhale.

It was getting late, though, so I took a Xanax, which I kept in my purse for PMS. Twenty-five milligrams, the lowest possible dose.

Not what they give crazy people.

I went back in the living room. I didn't want to call attention to Huey Long, so I tried to pick up the whole box of books, which was too heavy, so I slid the travel guides onto the floor and took the rest out to the car.

If I drive slowly and get caught in traffic, the Xanax will have kicked in by the time I get to Carter's. By the time I get home.

CARTER'S CAR WAS ALREADY THERE WHEN I pulled into the driveway behind him. The house looked like it always looked—yellow clapboard with white shutters, a white picket fence—but there was something strange and unfamiliar about it, like when you meet a person you've seen before but only in photographs and suddenly there's another dimension to them. It was an odd feeling, the opposite of déjà vu.

A little voice inside me was whispering, *Where are you and whose life are you suddenly living and how did you get here and how in hell do you get out?*

My hands were gripping the steering wheel so tight the blood was draining out of my fingertips, and I made myself let go and turn off the car and undo my seat belt. I shook my fingers and took a deep breath like a competitive diver getting ready to leap. I was moving to open the car door when Carter opened it for me and bent over to give me a quick kiss, which flustered me. I hadn't seen him come out of the house, so by the time I kissed him back, he'd already stood up and I found myself kissing air.

He said, "Welcome home," at the same time I said, "Hi," and I grabbed the box from the passenger seat, but he said, "No, let me get that."

I said, "It's all right," but he took it out of my arms.

We started walking toward the house.

I said, "How was your day?" mostly to keep him from asking me about the books.

"Like hell," he said, his favorite kind of workday.

I followed him down the brick footpath, and we passed his car and a flower bed and the trash bin while he told me about a guy on death row who was trying to get the Pope to ask my father to order a stay of execution.

"Tell me how much sense this makes," Carter said. "I left a hopeless marriage amicably and I'm about to marry the woman I want to spend the rest of my life with, so I won't be able to take communion, but if I'd stabbed and disemboweled two prostitutes, I'd have a shot at getting an audience with the Vatican."

He grew up Catholic, which he was still sort of mad about, and he'd been stewing all day. He was venting about the death penalty and mass media and mass stupidity as we headed around the house toward the back door, and I was making little sympathetic grunts, trying to sound like I was listening. It was cathartic for him, but it was getting me upset. I was against the death penalty and Carter wasn't, but I didn't want to get into that.

We went inside, into the kitchen. Something smelled funny, mildewy maybe, the way strangers' houses do when you're a child, an odor that says, *This is not where you belong.*

He'd been feeding his fish—a hundred-gallon saltwater tank of them—and an empty box of frozen Marine Cuisine sat on the counter.

Carter set the books on the floor by the refrigerator and said, "I'm sorry."

I thought he sensed something in me. I said, "It's not your fault." I put my purse on the counter.

He took my hand and said, "I mean all that talk about the Vatican, that's not how I wanted this to go."

I said, "Oh, okay, it's okay."

"What did you think I meant?"

"About what?"

"What isn't my fault?"

"Nothing."

"Wait a minute," he said.

I said, "That came out wrong."

He said, "Let's just start over."

"Yes."

He threw away the fish food box.

"I'm glad you're here," he said. "Welcome home."

I was glad to be there, too, I said. I heard us, sounding like lawyers at a tax litigation seminar.

He put his arms around me and held me tight, and I leaned into him and held onto him and tried to let go of everything else. I closed my eyes and pressed my face into his chest. The starch in his shirt against my skin smelled cool and clean and reminded me of my father—my father when I was a child, when he represented everything good and safe and barely beyond my reach in the world.

I opened my eyes. We'd had the kitchen remodeled—granite countertops that would last through a hurricane. I'd wanted to move, to get away from the memory of Carter's first wife and the residue of that marriage that started out as full of hope as anybody's does and ended in a bitter custody fight over a dog, but he loved that house. It was important to him to make something work there, his version of undoing bad karma, so we redid every room. Every floor, every wall, every light fixture and window treatment and bookshelf was exactly what I'd asked for, and I knew I should feel lucky or grateful or at least satisfied, but part of me missed that elusive comfort that comes when you look at your worn carpet and think, *Someday we'll replace that with a nicer color, and everything will be better.*

I stepped back, out of our embrace. I stood on my own two feet.

Carter had brought home pâté and French bread and a bottle of wine, and I sliced the bread while he opened the bottle. I got out two glasses and set them on the counter.

I was about to take his hand to go into the living room when he reached for a book in my box, and as his fingers passed over *Huey Long*, I felt that panic you get when something's about to spill, everything's going to be ruined.

He said, "What's this?" It was the book about past lives.

"Nothing," I said. "The past."

I took it from him, put it back in the box.

I said, "Pour me a glass of wine," and he turned away from the books.

He hadn't noticed *Huey Long*, or if he had, he didn't know what was inside it, and he acted like he hadn't heard the urgency in my voice. He wasn't picking up on anything I was feeling, which I was glad and sort of irritated about at the same time.

He started telling me about his day again as he poured the wine. Nutria—giant rodents that live in Louisiana swamps and destroy the ecosystems—and nutria fur and nutria meat and a nutria lobby that was trying to get a special tax break for supplying school hot-lunch programs with frozen nutria patties before they'd support my father in the next election. He said, "It's a good concept—just eat the fuckers—until you've got one on your plate."

I laughed, which came out sounding like I was choking.

He handed me my glass. I was trying to convince myself that my little panic had been normal everyday self-consciousness, like not wanting somebody to look in your medicine cabinet even if you don't have anything particularly embarrassing to hide.

We brought our wine and the bread and pâté into the living room, and I slipped off my shoes. The TV was on with the sound turned off but we weren't watching it. It was good, just being there together, being quiet. I was starting to get hungry, but I didn't eat any bread. I liked that feeling of uncomplicated physical desire—wanting something and knowing what it is you want and knowing that you're going to get it.

I drank to Carter and he touched my face and I kissed the palm of his hand. I liked that, too, the way it feels to drink a glass of wine with the man you love when the light is just beginning to change, the sun hanging heavy in the trees, darkness hovering just out of sight, and you can almost believe the world is about to be at peace.

Carter took my feet in his hands. He was using acupuncture pressure points to drain the tension, and I was feeling transparent and full of dark, liquid yearnings for things I couldn't name. I touched my forehead, pressed at the center of it with my middle finger.

Then I crawled into his lap, facing him, straddling him, and we drank to our engagement and our house—my new home—and our life together and my father's re-election campaign, which was just starting up, and every time we drank, we kissed. Then we toasted love and happiness and world peace and the colonization of Mars, and soon we were doing more kissing than drinking, and we set our empty glasses on the floor. We lay down together on the sofa, face to face, our bodies connected head to toe, and then we were still kissing, and he rolled me on top of him and his hands moved inside my clothes, hot on my back, and his touch flared bright inside my skin and my boundaries began to dissolve. I was moving out of myself into that space that opens up around you when the man you love is running his fingers like music over your body, and the laws that govern nature seem to lose their power and gravity loses its pull and time rushes on without you and the rest of the world fades into darkness. I was beginning to feel like the woman a magician levitates—one minute you're lying there being caressed, still and beautiful and sparkling, and the next minute you're floating in air, held in suspension by the power of desire, and the world becomes a holy place in a circle of light where love can hold you up.

Then he stopped.

He was still touching me, but something had stopped, as if the house lights came on and the spotlight turned off and whatever part of me that was rising started to fall.

He knows. He either knows about the video or he knows the same information that's on the video, but he knows more than I do.

I opened my eyes. He was watching TV. The sound was still off, but he'd turned the caption control on, and it was a commercial, a singing cartoon chicken. The caption had a little musical note beside the words "cluck cluck cluck," and my brain started listing words that rhymed with cluck.

I felt heavy and hot and stuck inside my body. His fingers were still moving absently over me, except now it was like when the magician passes his hands over the assistant as he sets her back on the table—he wasn't really touching me and I wasn't really floating, it was all an illusion, and whatever his hands were doing by then, it was just a distraction. I was still lying with him, on top of him.

When the commercial ended, the local news came on, a split screen, the anchor in the studio on one side and a still photo of my father, smiling, on the other.

I should give up now and get dressed.

But I didn't want it to go like that, didn't want to start a pattern, so I slipped off my panties and straddled his lap again and whispered, "You already know what he's going to say." He'd written the speech my father was about to give, read it to me in bed the night before. I pulled on his belt buckle.

I said, "Come on, he can't see us." Which wasn't exactly a joke, but I smiled as if it was and began to undress him. I touched him inside his clothes, and the light from my father's face flickered in the room, and I closed my eyes. I kissed him softly on the lips, and when he kissed me back, his breath was warm on my skin. I pulled him close, and soon, he came inside me and we were ignoring my father together. I was moaning softly. I pressed my chest to his chest and felt my voice moving there, inside him. I wasn't thinking about the video or my father. I was just feeling blissfully and desperately connected to Carter, or to that moment together in time, and therefore separate from the rest of the world and safe.

Then I heard the voice of the local news anchor. I opened my eyes in a question, and Carter was still inside my blouse, inside me, touching my back with one hand but holding the remote control in the other, and he said, "I'm sorry, this will just take a second, but I've got to hear this."

I moved to get off his lap, but he put his hands on my thighs and said, "Please, just wait."

I didn't want to argue about it, not there and not then, so I leaned over to pick up my glass, but of course it was still empty.

I thought about pouring myself another. I considered tucking in my blouse and pulling on my panties and my shoes and leaving and not coming back, but I just sat there.

Carter was shrinking inside me, which didn't feel like shrinking, it felt like it was metamorphosing into something that belonged in a fish tank, so I looked over my shoulder to watch what Carter was watching, and I saw my father. I felt my hunger turning into anger, a dark, grasping feeling deep in my stomach.

Carter slipped out of me, limp.

I thought, *At least my father doesn't arouse him.*

Which I knew even at the time was an odd thought to comfort myself with.

I was thinking of my mother.

I'm okay, but if I were emotionally fragile to start with and I'd been treated like this for the last thirty-seven years—as long as my parents were married—I can see how I might just kill myself one night over nothing in particular.

15

Which was how I understood her death at the time.

I slid off Carter and sat on the floor, straightening my clothes. I hooked my bra.

Carter's eyes didn't move from the TV. He was a carbon copy of my father in a lot of ways, mostly because he modeled himself after my father, who modeled himself after a combination of Huey Long, JFK, Machiavelli, and Jesus Christ. Both Carter and my father were so driven by their belief in their own visions that they could look straight through the pain they caused the people they loved and see only beauty. It was the same kind of paradoxical instinct that leads a hunter who loves nature to pull a trigger on a dove in flight.

A bouquet of microphones bloomed at my father's chin, and Audrey, my mother's sister, my father's second wife, stood by his side. A month before, two months after my mother's death—way too soon, in my opinion—they'd gotten married.

When Carter began to whisper the speech with my father from memory, I pulled on my panties under my skirt.

I BARELY SLEPT ALL NIGHT, BUT BY THE time I woke up the next morning, Carter had already left for work. I pulled a robe on over my nightgown and went in the kitchen, where he'd left coffee for me, and poured myself a cup.

Huey Long still sat in the box by the refrigerator, small and inert and harmless, and I suddenly felt embarrassed by it, my reaction to it the day before. I took a sip of coffee and tightened my robe around me.

I still had a bad feeling. If I'd lived in California, I would have thought I was having an earthquake premonition and I would have gone to a doorway to drink my coffee, but being in Baton Rouge, where all natural disasters come with warnings from the National Weather Service, I just walked around the house. I put my hands on the kitchen table, left my fingerprints there. I went in the living room. I picked up books and pillows and candlestick holders and put them back down in slightly different places. I nudged the second hand on the clock. I went in Carter's study, where his pictures looked like they'd been hung by an army sergeant, and bumped a few of them into slight angles.

It was the opposite of what I did before I told Ray I wanted a divorce. Then, I went through every room in our condo, looking at all the things I'd lived with for so long I'd stopped seeing them. I moved the books from my bedside table back to the shelves. I straightened pictures and emptied the dishwasher and adjusted the runner in the hall. I dusted. I put everything where it belonged, and afterward, I asked myself one last time if I could find a way to belong there, too. Then I tried to figure out what I wanted to keep, what I'd be willing to lose, and found out I didn't want any of it. That was how I decided to leave, by realizing I couldn't stay.

I went back in the kitchen and put my coffee cup in the sink. I was going to get a book out of my box and put it on the bedside table when I realized what else I was doing—delaying the inevitable.

I checked the lock on the kitchen door.

I looked out the window to make sure Carter's car was gone.

I got the video out of the book and put the book back in the box, exactly where it had been before.

Then I walked down the hall and into the bedroom, put the tape in the VCR, turned on the TV and VCR, and sat on the edge of the bed. A soap opera came on, a beautiful woman in a prison cell with a perfect makeup job and messy hair screaming for a guard.

My fingers were trembling when I pressed PLAY.

At first there was just static, then horizontal lines, and then a chair, an empty armchair beside an empty fireplace. I'd seen it before, though I didn't place it instantly. Then the torso of a woman fiddling with the camera, and then time went all out of joint—it was my mother.

I pressed STOP, and the prisoner came back on, crying now, and I pressed MUTE.

I wasn't sure I was ready to hear what my mother had to say.

If this was important, why not just tell me while she was still alive? Why not leave a suicide note like normal people? Or if she just had to do it this way, why not leave the tape for my father instead of me?

I took a deep breath.

It's creepy, and it's cruel, sending a message like this from the grave where no matter what she says, what she needs, what kind of pain she's in, there's no way I'll be able to respond.

My chest was aching and so was my arm, but I wasn't having a heart attack.

I said to myself, *It's okay, she can't hurt you anymore. It's all over.*

Which was the part that hurt the most.

I pressed at my heart like I was singing the national anthem, which sometimes helped although not that time.

A commercial for laundry detergent came on, animated clothes twisting in a washing machine, cartoon stains disappearing like ghosts. All the reasons I didn't have to watch her and all the reasons I did were spinning around together in my head like laundry.

Maybe this is what it feels like to be crazy. You have the same thoughts everybody else does, but yours keep tangling themselves up in each other until you can't tell where one ends and the next begins.

I was afraid of ending up like my mother—manic depression is a highly hereditary illness—but I didn't want to think about myself anymore, so I turned the tape back on.

She was wearing her favorite pink suit, the Jackie Kennedy suit with the pink leather pumps she wore the day my father took the oath of office. It was tight on her now, she'd put on weight since the inauguration. I thought she'd never worn that suit again—she kept it preserved in a cedar chest in the attic, thinking some museum might ask for it—and it's the suit I would have had her buried in, though my father had her cremated wearing, as far as I knew, only the nightgown she had on when she died. I didn't ask. Maybe they cremate everyone naked, so they don't have to deal with zippers and buttons and flame-resistant chemicals in certain fabrics, but I didn't want to know. I didn't want to think about it, and I didn't want to imagine it, though of course I had, vividly, many times—*her hair lifts up with the flames, her face opens into the wide-eyed grin of a bare-boned skull, and she burns and she burns until her bones collapse in on themselves, glowing.*

She was sitting in the chair by the fireplace in the master bedroom at the Mansion like everything was normal, like presidents do for fireside chats on TV to tell the country that we've gone to war but it's nothing to worry about. She wasn't exactly smiling, but she was calm, and she'd done her hair and makeup like she always did, when she did them at all. She wasn't crying. She was just sitting there in the chair by the empty fireplace with her hands folded in her lap like she was about to make a public service announcement—*buckle up, Louisiana*—and what was terrifying about it was its sheer banality.

My hands felt heavy and my arms felt heavy and I felt a heavy pressing in my throat like you get before you cry—all the unspoken, unspeakable things I wanted to say to her. Then I felt a pulling in my chest—the things I'd never hear her say to me.

She cleared her throat and I swallowed hard.

"I'm not sure this thing is working," she said. Her voice sounded fragile and far away, like she wasn't getting enough air, or she'd tasted something bitter, like poison. Though she died in New Orleans, so I knew she wasn't dying as she spoke.

I won't have to watch her die.

"I don't know how to tell," she said, and her voice began to find its footing. "Which has been my problem all my life. I never knew if the medicine was working, or the marriage, or even the car."

Then she laughed once, almost, a hard thud of a laugh that seemed to jar something loose, and her words started tumbling out in a rush. "I'd take it into the shop and say it's making a noise and they'd say nothing's wrong with it, lady, it's all in your head. Then they'd charge me a hundred dollars and send me home, and one day it just died on me in a puddle, a three-inch-deep puddle, which I thought was significant at the time. I didn't mean to get off on it now, though."

She stopped and looked at the ceiling and took a deep breath.

I was trying to breathe, too.

She looked back at the camera, at me, and opened her hands like a wordless book and looked at them. She cocked her head, as if she was surprised to find them empty. Then she closed them together. She put one hand on each arm of the chair and held on tight, like an astronaut just before takeoff, an inmate in the electric chair.

"Well, the red light is on," she said, speaking more tentatively, "so maybe it's working. Or maybe the red light means stop, stop talking. Everybody's always trying to get me to stop talking and I'm about to, but I've got one more thing to say and no goddamn red light is going to stop me. Remember when we went to the red light district in Amsterdam, and red meant go? And the pretty prostitutes just stood in their doorways under the red lights, waiting, but the ugly ones had to dress themselves up in chains and artificial body parts, and when the men went in they'd close the door, or is that when they turned on the red lights? I don't remember. But see, that's how all of life is. The pretty ones get everything if they wait long enough. Oh yes they do. But I've gotten off on another jag here I didn't mean to get off on. I'm not concentrating too well. It might be the medicine. So I'll get straight to the point."

She glanced at the ceiling and blinked—I couldn't tell if she was trying not to cry or just looking for words—then she leaned in toward the camera and lowered her voice: "They're trying to kill me."

She let go of her grip on the chair and started rubbing the fabric, back and forth, back and forth, with her fingertips.

"I think they're drugging me," she said, "pills that blur my mind, or downers, trying to drive me to suicide. They've got drugs that can do that. They've got drugs that can do anything these days, just about anything, only they can't make you happy. They can't make somebody love you if he doesn't, and that's the pill everybody's always wanted."

I was sort of reeling inside my head.

Be logical. One, there's no such thing as a drug that can drive you to suicide. Who would make such a drug? Who would test it? Who would insure the company that sold it? So that's it, she's being paranoid, afraid of her own suicidal thoughts, which makes sense because who wouldn't be if they heard their own brain telling them they'd be better off dead?

I wasn't suicidal, but I couldn't say I'd never had a suicidal thought, and I knew it was scary as hell.

Every thought and feeling is a chemical action or reaction in the brain, and when your chemicals aren't right, you can have thoughts that feel so foreign to who you are that you might think you were being drugged, but that wouldn't mean it was true.

"Everybody's always wanting what they can't have," she said. "It's the oldest story there is, the Garden of Eden and the Kama Sutra and all of Greek tragedy, which is not the point. I should rewind this and take that out, but I've tried to do this before and I'm running out of time. If I start trying to edit myself now I'll never finish. So I just want to clarify what I mean about the Kama Sutra because a regular human body can't bend into eighty percent of those positions, I've tried. Which is not exactly relevant and more than I meant to say, probably more than anybody wanted to know, but I didn't like it hanging there unexplained. This is what always happens. Shit."

Her feet started fidgeting and she was restless, almost rocking as if she wanted to leave, but she held on to the chair to keep herself there.

I was frozen to the bed, holding on to the remote control, trying to make her stay in her chair and keep talking. I wanted to put my hands out and touch her, hold her, but of course she wasn't really there, and I wished I weren't there either, wished it were a tape of me sitting there while the real me was off somewhere else, oblivious, or even dead.

She looked over her shoulder, jerked her head as if she was afraid somebody had just come in the room, but there was nothing behind her.

I suddenly got that feeling you get on the back of your neck when you're being watched, and I looked over my shoulder thinking maybe Carter had snuck back in the house and seen the whole thing, but I was still alone, too. I looked back at her.

She put her hands over her ears and pressed her head the way she did with certain kinds of headaches and looked at the floor.

"First, I tried to write this down," she said, still looking at her feet. "I was trying to show what it's like, what I hear, what I think, but I get a pen in my hand and it's like the pen sucks the words out of my brain, or the connecting words, the ones that make it make sense. It's like somebody's planted brain-sucking pens everywhere in this place, which is another story, but here's my point." She looked up at the camera again. "I heard them," she said. "I heard their voices through the door. And I'm not talking about hearing voices, I'm talking about people who were plotting to kill me. A lot of women have ended up dead because they didn't believe their own husband would kill them, but then, of course, he did. And at first I didn't believe it either. I couldn't, because people say things like,'I could just kill her' every day, but nobody means it. Or almost nobody does. So then you realize what's really happening, that it's literally true, and what all the things you've tried to ignore over the months and years really meant, and it kills you. It just kills you right there. So you're walking around dead in your body, and the rest is just details. Of course, if Saint Augustine was right and God is in the details, well, that explains a thing or two. I'm not sure what."

She crossed her legs.

"I can't even say this right. I'm not saying this right. I don't know how to. Nobody ever tells you how to do something like this. There should be a class, a self-help book, because you feel like you're the only one who's ever been where you are, but the sad thing is, everybody who ever got here felt that way."

She uncrossed her legs and closed her eyes tight. Then she moved her hands to cover her face. She was giving up, and her voice was breaking, broken. She shook her head.

"I don't blame Audrey," she said. "I blame him. Maybe it's my own fault, but I can't keep living this way. I can't keep living, never knowing what's going on behind closed doors, and all the staff running around the house baking bread, offering me coffee, drugged coffee, for all I know—how do you trust a bunch of murderers?—so my own home is a prison but I feel like I'm the prisoner, we're all just prisoners here."

Then her hands fell to her lap and she looked at the camera.

"That's a song, isn't it? I guess there's nothing left to say that hasn't been said already in a song. God, that's pathetic."

She laughed another bitter, one-syllable laugh and shook her head again, but this time it was a relaxed gesture, full of irony. Something in her changed, as if something had been released, or decided, or finished. She crossed her legs again and leaned back as if she were comfortable, and her hands relaxed on the arms of the chair.

"It keeps coming back to this," she said, and her tone was almost casual now. "Every person on that staff is a murderer. Most of them killed their wives. Or lovers. Or their wives' lovers."

This part, at least, wasn't as crazy as it sounded. The Mansion was staffed by trusties from the state prison, all serving life sentences for crimes of passion, and usually, almost by definition, crimes of passion that receive life sentences are killings motivated by sexual jealousy.

She said, "So I'm asking, once you've killed your own wife, what's the big deal about killing somebody else's?"

She has a point.

The logic behind the policy was that people who commit crimes of passion are less likely to commit other offenses on the job than, for example, drug dealers, sex offenders, or thieves. Though it also stands to reason that they'd be more likely than your average prisoner to commit murder.

"Think about it," she said. "He can pardon them or send them back to Angola just by saying,'Let there be light.' He's God Almighty as far as they're concerned, so if he says to the butler, for example,'Put one of these in my wife's coffee,' you tell me what's to stop him."

She started tensing up again. She smoothed the fabric arms of the chair with her palms, as if there were huge wrinkles in them.

"The butler's never going to tell," she said, "because for one thing, who would believe him? If he says a word to anybody and I end up dead, he just brings all the suspicion on himself. It's the perfect crime. Really, I almost admire it."

She stopped and shook her head and exhaled a smile.

Then she furrowed her eyebrows and looked at the floor and her mouth fell open and her body sort of slumped, as if her muscles had stopped working.

After a moment, she said, "Where was I?" to no one in particular. She wasn't looking at the camera. She didn't even seem aware of it. She was muttering, talking to herself, staring at the floor.

She said, "This didn't come out right, but I can't go through it again. I used to think, who wouldn't fight a thing like this with every bone in her body? But once you accept the one thing you thought would never happen as possible, black could be white, up could be down, good could be evil, life feels like death. All the walls come down, all the boundaries that keep one thing from being its opposite, and the world of possibilities has a whole different shape. So you can believe just about anything. I don't mean as in, you'll believe anything because you're gullible. More like you'll believe anything because you're . . . well, *not* gullible anymore. Not crazy, where you don't know real from unreal. It's just—I don't know. I've gotten off track again. Dammit."

Then she turned to the side and looked away for a long time. Her expression was blank, as if she was seeing nothing. She sniffed and let out a long breath.

I waited to see if there was more—I needed more, I needed a lot more—but then she shook her head and whispered, "I'm sorry."

She stood up and walked back toward the camera, leaving the empty chair.

I closed my eyes and waited.

I counted to ten.

Then I counted to twenty.

She was fiddling with the camera.

Then there was just static, and she was gone.

I would have kept waiting—I was still waiting, in a way—but I knew she wasn't coming back. My hands were knotted into fists, and I opened them and looked at them. They were empty.

I missed my mother the way you miss color in winter in Ohio, so badly you could almost cut yourself open just to see red.

I sat for a long time staring at the static, listening to it, taking it in. I felt it move hot up my spine and divide itself into horizontal lines in my brain, then flicker into thought: *How do you face the possibility that the man you've loved most in the world, or at least most desperately, the person you've needed most and resented most for not giving you what you needed, the one you've admired and feared and emulated and rebelled*

*from and run to and trusted with your heart and your body and your soul—
how do you face the possibility that the man who gave you life also killed your
mother?*

It's not the same as asking how you look at the face of evil. It's
not nearly that simple.

It's like asking how you look at the face of God. And the Old Testament writers knew the answer: you don't. You can't. If you did, it would destroy you.

So you look at what you *can* see. You look at what could destroy you but doesn't. Moses looked at a burning bush, knowing he wasn't seeing God but believing he'd heard Him. And the Israelites followed a pillar of clouds by day and a pillar of fire by night, believing the clouds and the fire were leading them where God, who remained invisible, wanted them to go. And somehow they came away from those encounters whole and unharmed, believing they'd seen and heard the truth.

I told myself, *If I can make myself look directly at the possibility that my father murdered my mother, I will see with certainty that he didn't. Approach the fire that could destroy you. Trust it, listen to it, follow it. And it won't burn.*

So this is how, the morning I watched my mother's video, I reconstructed her death:

It was Fat Tuesday, the last day of Mardi Gras. We'd all planned to meet that night for drinks at the Fairmont, my parents, Carter's parents, and Carter and I, but when my father arrived alone, I wasn't surprised. I was angry. My mother didn't like his parents, never had, and she hated that kind of event, avoided them when she could, but I thought she should have made an exception that night for my sake. It was the first time we'd tried to get our parents together since we'd started dating. I was also irritated at myself, though, at the part of me that felt relieved she wasn't there so I didn't have to look after her, didn't need to worry about her drinking too much and laughing uncontrollably, or crying.

Carter asked if everything was all right.

Without looking at him, my father said, "Marie's not feeling her best, but she'll be fine." Then he ordered a round of Sazeracs.

Even in retrospect, there was nothing sinister, nothing unusual, in my father's voice. If I had thought anything of that little exchange, I would only have wondered why Carter asked the question—he knew as well as I did how my mother was—but I assumed he was being polite. He was.

Carter's mother said, "What a pity," and downed her drink. From her point of view, we were their guests at the most important social event of the year, and the only thing that had happened was that she'd been snubbed.

I was facing a ten-foot-high mural of Huey Long and Ella Fitzgerald and some other famous dead people I didn't recognize. Huey used to drink there, used to govern the state from his suite there, wearing white silk pajamas and entertaining beautiful young women and destroying the lives and careers of everybody who opposed him while his wife stayed at home, out of sight. The parallels between Huey and my father had always made me uncomfortable. That's where my mind was.

The men were dressed in white ties and tails at the bar, but like all Rex krewe members, Carter's father came to the ball masked, wearing a gold lamé cape with gold knickers and gold tights. Before the dancing began, a military band played patriotic hymns while a dozen twenty-year-old coeds dressed in white lined up to approach the krewe one by one, lowering their heads and curtsying until their knees touched the floor: pseudo-virgins offering themselves to rich, white, pseudo-royal pseudo-superheroes, all without a trace of irony. I thought my feelings at that point did more to explain my mother's absence than raise questions about it: I was sort of wishing I'd skipped the evening with her.

Once, I said to Carter, "It wouldn't have killed my mother to come say hello."

He barely twitched—or maybe I made that up after the fact—but then he acted like he hadn't heard me. And maybe he hadn't. It was a loud room. Or maybe he was doing what my father does in press conferences when a reporter asks him a question he doesn't want to answer. He turned away from me as if he hadn't heard me, shook a man's hand, and asked him how he was doing without introducing me.

We didn't mention my mother the rest of the evening. I didn't even think of her, didn't bother to check on her when I went to bed.

Audrey was there with an openly gay man, a writer friend of hers, laughing at everything he said and touching his hands like she wanted people to think they were on a real date. She kept her distance from us, where she was usually the moth to my father's flame, but I didn't stop to wonder why. I was just glad not to have to deal with her. That was how I was living my life, on a need-to-know basis, and I didn't think I needed to know anything more about Audrey at that point than I did.

My father went out of his way to shake the hand of every millionaire in the room. He knew all their names, accepted all their invitations to go hunting or deep-sea fishing with them. He talked boats and lures and rifles and ammunitions with them and laughed hard and loud at their jokes. There was nothing unusual in the way he looked or acted or spoke. He was working—he was always working— laying his groundwork to raise money to run for President.

My mother's absence was a reminder of the still, I assumed, unanswered question of what to do about her if he got the party's nomination. He could run for Governor without her help, but in a presidential campaign, her absence would have been almost as much of a liability as her presence, though I was willing and eager to fill in some of that gap. I thought we could have worked something out. Chances were, though, he wouldn't get the nomination— for one thing, nobody from Louisiana ever had—and it would be a moot point.

After the ball, my father, Carter, and Carter's father went off to the Boston Club to smoke cigars with some other krewe members, and Carter's mother and I went to our rooms in the hotel, where I watched some TV and fell asleep.

When I woke up, Carter was back. He'd turned off the TV and was brushing his teeth. He was still wearing his tails, but I didn't think anything of it. I wasn't thinking yet, I was groggy. Normally, the three or four nights we'd spent together at that point, he'd put on his pajamas first, then brush his teeth, but if I had thought about it, I would have figured it was the cigars, that he wanted to get the taste out of his mouth, not that he knew something. Not that he knew, for example, that there was no point in getting undressed because my mother was dead and my father was about to call us to her bedside. And although he wasn't surprised when the phone rang, as I was—it was past three in the morning—he'd just come in, so it might not have seemed odd to him for somebody to call with one more joke, one more political jab.

He picked up the phone and said, "Yeah," though he usually says hello like everybody else, but his mouth was full of toothpaste. His voice sounded edgy, anxious—I noticed that even at the time—but smoking always makes him hoarse.

But when he said, "Hold on," and without looking at me, dropped the phone on the bed and went in the bathroom to spit, I knew something was wrong. I sat up wanting to know who was calling at that hour and why, but he didn't even look my way, so I could have picked up the phone and asked who it was myself, but I knew enough to know I didn't want to know more.

When he came back and picked up the phone again, there almost wasn't time for my father to say, for example, "She's dead"—there was hardly time for him to say anything at all—before Carter said, "We'll be right there."

Though maybe there was time. He didn't need that much and I wasn't clocking it. I just felt like things suddenly sped up too fast to make sense because Carter hung up and said, "It's your mother. Get dressed," and something in his voice made me do it fast without asking questions. I pulled on my jeans, left my pajama top on, and we ran down the hall into the elevator and the doors slid shut and we were alone and Carter pressed the button for the Concierge floor. The elevator started moving—I could feel it lurch in my stomach up to my throat—and Carter kept pressing the button again and again, breathing too hard. He smelled of cigars, an anxious, angry smell.

I was scared.

I looked down at the floor, trying to calm myself, and saw I was bleeding. I was barefoot and somebody had dropped his drink on the elevator floor and I'd run in without looking and stepped on the glass, though I hadn't felt the cut when it happened. I picked up a piece of ice, figuring it still had some alcohol on it—I wasn't thinking clearly—and rubbed it on the wound.

Carter still wouldn't look at me. I told myself he couldn't stand the sight of blood, so I watched him watch the floor numbers light up, pressing the DOOR CLOSED button as if that would make us get there faster.

Finally, I said, "What did she say?"

He shook his head and said, "Oh, no. I'm sorry. It was your father who called. Your mother's—"

Then he stopped, and something had been rushing hard and cold through me like panic, and it stopped.

I should have said, "What about her?" I should have covered my face with my hands or asked him to hold me or banged my fist on the wall of the elevator or said a silent prayer—I don't know what I should have done, what is anybody supposed to do in that situation?—but I should have done something, and I didn't. I did absolutely nothing. I stood very still where I was, not moving a muscle, and I looked at the elevator floor. It was marble with long streaks running through it like fault lines, cracks that could break open and we'd fall straight through.

I dropped the ice and whispered, "No."

I knew she was dead.

Later, the thought would cross my mind that I knew because Carter knew: *What if he'd been holding in his chest the shapeless secret of what would happen, and he knew he could let part of it go as soon as we got to her room, but he let it go early, exhaled it, and it hung heavy in the tight elevator air, and I breathed it in like secondhand smoke, and then I knew it, too?*

But it wasn't that. It was common sense. The phone never brings good news in the middle of the night.

Or maybe I remember knowing she was dead because it's what turned out to be true. Maybe whatever had happened, three months after the fact, moments after watching my mother's video, I would have thought to myself, *I knew it.*

But whatever our reasons, when we got to the room, neither Carter nor I acted surprised. My father opened the door, and my fifty-seven-year-old mother lay dead in the bed with her eyes wide open, her face looking very white and very fragile and strangely peaceful.

She'd been living for so many years with so much anger and hurt, pain in every muscle, every layer of skin, rage over rage over rage like masks, that when all the tension was suddenly gone, what was left was this delicate, beautiful woman I'd never seen before. It was an astonishing sight, but it wasn't surprising at all. It was almost as if something that was lost had been restored, but none of us had realized it was gone until it was back.

We all stood there for a long time, staring at her. And none of us tried CPR. None of us called 911. Nobody wept.

I've never seen my father weep, but I looked in his eyes to see if he had, even briefly, when he came in from partying all night and found his wife dead. He hadn't.

I wasn't weeping either. My mother was the one who expressed all the emotions in the family. I didn't know what my father was feeling, and I couldn't tell if what I was feeling was grief or guilt for my lack of grief or anger at my father for his lack of grief or anger at Carter just for being there, for knowing before I did, knowing more than I did. And maybe the truth was, I was relieved. I had to face that possibility. It was true that I'd begun to feel exhausted by her and unappreciated and trapped. Or maybe it was just shock. The emotional equivalent of snow was floating inside me, something cold and white and silent and calm as night falling in my head, blanketing me away from myself.

My father said he thought it was probably either a heart attack or a stroke. He was speaking softly, as if he didn't want to disturb her.

Carter said it could have been a brain aneurysm, he remembered my mother mentioning headaches.

I didn't remember any such thing, but it didn't raise a question in me. I'd gotten to where I didn't listen to her every complaint.

My father took a sip of whatever he was drinking. His glass was still full.

There was an empty bottle of vodka and some empty vials of prescription pills on the table by the bed, though at that moment their obvious meaning hadn't processed its way through my head. I was still wading through an internal blizzard where nothing, not even my own thought, seemed to hold its shape.

I was trying to understand my father's reaction, though I had no frame of reference for what an appropriate response from any of us would have been. The way I figured it, my father and Carter had come back from the Boston Club together—they went there together—and my father had found my mother about the same time Carter came in our room—a little later, since my father was on the top floor—and called us instantly and poured himself a drink while he waited for us. So he'd had only a few extra minutes to get used to the fact that she was dead.

I thought, *He's adjusting very quickly. Too quickly, maybe, but then, he's a practical man.*

I was, I thought, adjusting quickly, too.

Then he leaned over her body and gently closed her eyes with his thumbs. It was the first time I'd seen him touch her in a very long time, and whatever had kept me from knowing what I felt when I first saw her was gone, melted instantly away like Louisiana snow, and I knew exactly what I felt: I hated my mother. I hated her for doing what she'd done and for not doing what she hadn't done, for taking what she'd taken and giving the hell she'd given. I hated myself for putting up with her, for sympathizing with her, loving her, and I wanted my father to touch me. I wanted him to close my eyes. I wanted that gentleness, that glimpse of kindness, for myself. I wanted it deep in my body, in my bones, the way you want to be warm when you're so freezing cold that nothing else matters.

Carter said in a hushed voice that she didn't look like she'd been in any pain. Then he carefully closed her suitcase.

My father said, "She's cold. She must have been gone for several hours." Then he put her arms under the covers. He picked up her hands, her beautiful, delicate, manicured hands, and her arms moved easily, they hadn't begun to stiffen—I didn't know how long that would take—and he placed them at her sides and smoothed the sheets over her lovingly, as if he were tucking a child into bed for the night.

I just stood there, looking around the room, not doing a thing.

It was a suite with a living room and a stocked kitchen, and everything was mahogany and glass and thick beige fabric. It was clean without feeling antiseptic, elegant without being stuffy, comfortable but impersonal. Private. Which was how her death felt to me at that point.

I was thinking, *He's not going to touch my face.*

I knew that.

He won't touch me at all, not until I'm dead.

We'd never been very demonstrative with each other—he never even tucked me into bed when I was a child except when I pretended to fall asleep in the car so he'd have to carry me to my room—and there was no reason to think my mother's death would change that. I touched my own face, pressed my fingers to my eyelids until I saw lights twinkling in the distance inside me.

My father said, "We'll just say she died of natural causes in the press release," as if he was planning already to avoid an autopsy.

Carter said he'd take care of it—though technically he was just my father's speech writer at the time, not his press secretary—which I thought was an act of kindness to me. I'd quit my job at the Louisiana Film Commission six months before so she could get the daily care she needed without the press finding out, and clearly I'd failed.

She killed herself while I was supposed to be looking out for her, and they're both trying to protect me because it's my fault.

My father was taking the bottles off the bedside table and dropping them into the plastic hotel laundry bag.

I felt myself floating up out of my skin. I couldn't connect my mother to the body lying there dead on the bed and I couldn't connect myself to the person who'd let her do it. I wanted to hold her, to shake the life back into her and pick her up in my arms and carry her to a place where she'd be safe and warm and alive, a place I could love her and she could love me and where love would matter. But I couldn't get my feet to move.

Carter was hanging up my mother's clothes next to her ball gown with the tags still on it. I wouldn't think anything of it until later, when the questions raced through me. Although she might have bought the gown just to keep my father from suspecting her plans, like buying time. She might have paid a fortune for it, just for spite, knowing he wouldn't get the bill until after she was gone. She might have bought it a long time ago. She'd have days where she'd buy anything that was for sale. She might have bought it because she wasn't thinking clearly.

Or, she might have planned to wear it.

My foot had stopped bleeding, but I'd tracked it onto the carpet, each mark smaller and lighter than the one before, as if I'd gradually disappeared. Neither Carter nor my father seemed to have noticed. I was trying not to notice what they were doing either, but I couldn't shake the feeling that we were messing up a crime scene and I was going to end up a suspect because my blood was on the carpet.

So I told myself, *I'm being irrational, I'm just in shock.*

Which I was.

Then my father handed me the laundry bag and said, "Take care of this, Grayson."

I took the bag because I didn't want it to fall on the floor, but I didn't say anything. I wasn't sure what he was asking me to do, and I thought he'd tell me, but he didn't, and he didn't wait for an answer.

Then he turned to Carter and said, "Do you think we should call the police?" though my father never asked anybody for advice.

Carter immediately said, "I don't see any reason to."

I was about to offer my opinion—she was my mother, after all—but I still wasn't thinking at normal speed and couldn't come up with an opinion to offer before my father asked Carter, "Should we call an ambulance?"

Carter said, "She wouldn't want that. You've got media listening in to all calls that go out to ambulances and the police, and the last thing we want now is television cameras filming the body being taken out of the hotel."

All of which my father surely already knew, but he said, "I agree, we want to avoid a media circus, let her have a little peace. Let's call Mike Fontenot," his personal physician, though it was obviously far too late for a doctor.

They were acting like I wasn't there, but something about the way they talked, the flatness of their voices, maybe, or the way they answered each other without even pausing to think what to say, or maybe it was the fact that they were dressed exactly alike, in white ties and tails, like vaudeville performers—something made me feel like what was happening wasn't real. They were working from a script, and they already knew what they were going to do with the body, which was just a prop, and it was only for my benefit that they were discussing it as if they didn't, and they were about to burst into song.

I thought, *Maybe I just made that up. Obviously I did—they're not about to sing. So they're talking this way because they're in shock, too, and they've gone into a kind of automatic pilot, and I have this feeling that something is wrong because something is wrong, but what it is, is that my mother is dead.*

They were discussing how to get the body—that's how they referred to her, as *the body*—how to get her out of the hotel without taking her out the main entrance where she might be photographed. Carter said he'd noticed a service elevator.

I suddenly felt furious at them both, but the focus of my fury at that moment was that she wouldn't have wanted to make her last exit out the back door. She didn't need to. People go to a lot of trouble during Mardi Gras to make themselves look dead; they dress in tattered shrouds and make themselves up to look like they're bleeding and decomposing and they build Styrofoam coffins and tombstones and strap them to their backs and drink themselves into stupors, so by Fat Tuesday night, you could drag her through the lobby, and if anybody noticed that she looked dead, their only thought would be that she didn't look dead enough. But I couldn't say all that, I didn't have the words, and I felt weak under the weight of all that wasn't being said, and I let the laundry bag fall to the floor as I lay down on the bed.

I was lying with my mother.

I curled up next to her and rested my head on her chest, her cold, still chest, and I felt cold and deathly still myself and barely there. I could hear the absence of her heartbeat in my ear the way you hear the absence of clocks humming in your house when the lights go out and it feels like time itself has stopped and the quiet suddenly makes you aware of the sound of your own breathing and the weight of your soul.

I don't know how long I lay there or what Carter and my father did during that time, but when I opened my eyes, they were both looking at me. Their faces were completely expressionless. I blinked and looked back at them. It felt like time was starting up again, slowly, and we'd all just realized I was still there.

My father picked up the laundry bag off the floor and held it out to me and said, "Okay. Now go on."

I sat up, suddenly embarrassed, as if I'd been caught reading my mother's diary. Or looking at her naked, touching her where her clothes should have been. It was that kind of physical privacy I'd violated, though I don't mean it in a sexual way. I never heard her heartbeat when she was alive.

I looked at the bag in my father's hands and took it. Then I looked at it in my own hands. Carter handed me the room key, and I left.

I was thirty-four years old and I'd been divorced for three years, but for some reason, I hadn't wanted my father to know Carter and I were sleeping together. There it was, though, and it didn't seem like a revelation, and it didn't seem to matter. Lots of things suddenly didn't matter.

In the elevator, I tried to drink the last of the vodka, but it was all gone. Then it hit me, what I was doing—trying to finish off the liquor my mother had used to kill herself. I put the bottle back in the bag.

I looked around. My foot was suddenly throbbing. I was afraid I'd left a sliver of glass in it that could get in an artery and travel to my brain. My whole body started throbbing so hard I thought I might be having a stroke, but I tried, from a lifetime of training, to act like nothing was wrong. I looked at the ceiling. I had a feeling the elevator was being videotaped for security, though I didn't see a camera.

When I got to my floor, I left the vodka bottle on a room-service tray outside somebody else's door at the other end of the hall. Then I went to my room. When I looked in the mirror, I could see my nipples through my top, and I pulled on a sweatshirt. Then I peeled the labels off the prescription bottles, tore them into shreds, and flushed them down the toilet. I rinsed and dried the bottles, put them back in the laundry bag, slipped on some tennis shoes, and stomped on the bottles with my good foot until they were crushed. On my way back to my father's room, I stuffed them into the built-in wastebasket by the elevator.

I knocked softly on my father's door, and Carter answered instantly. He stood in the doorway, not exactly blocking me from entering but not really welcoming me in either. I looked in the room, over Carter's shoulder. Dr. Fontenot was there, standing over my mother's body, still wearing his tails, not doing anything. My father was sitting in a chair, drinking. Dr. Fontenot crossed himself, and Carter looked at my father, and my father looked away.

I didn't know what was going to happen, but whatever it was, I didn't want to see it.

I left again without saying anything to any of them, and none of them lifted a finger to stop me.

I went out of the hotel, wandered past cops sitting on horses, street-cleaning machines moving through alleys like steamrollers, and mounds and mounds of garbage—beer cans and paper bags and plastic breasts and broken glass lying in heaps. I crossed Canal, where beads hung from the trees like sparkling Spanish moss, and went into the Quarter. Down a side street, an old woman surrounded by candles was shuffling cards. The moon was out, and the air smelled of pot and piss and sounded eerily quiet. I'd never been in the Quarter without hearing music somewhere, but the bars were closed and the revelers were in bed and the musicians had packed up their instruments and turned out the lights.

By early morning, I was standing in front of St. Louis Cathedral. When the priest opened the doors for the first Ash Wednesday services, I filed in behind the hungover believers. And while they found their places in the pews, I knelt on a prie-dieu and slipped a dollar into the locked offering box and lit a candle for my mother.

The sanctuary wasn't dark, but it wasn't bright. It was neither warm nor cold. The flame from the candle didn't seem to glow with light or heat or hope or the spirit of God. I had a feeling that whatever it was supposed to do, it wasn't doing it.

I could smell incense burning, and I tried to say a prayer for her, but I couldn't think what to pray. It seemed a little late for that. Then I tried to say one for myself, but I didn't feel right praying for myself when I couldn't pray for her. I knew it wouldn't work anyway as long as I didn't believe it would.

So I stayed there on the kneeling bench, resting. I'd been walking for hours, and my feet hurt.

An older man in a suit came in and knelt next to me. He was praying in French, whispering, wearing what looked at first glance like Mardi Gras beads, though of course it was a rosary. A picture started painting itself in my head of a bunch of men on a balcony, yelling, "Show me your tits!" and throwing rosaries to anybody who did. Then I put Jesus on the balcony, yelling, "Show me your broken heart!" and women started opening their blouses, exposing flaming hearts wrapped in thorns like barbed wire.

I told myself it was my fault, not God's, that my prayers weren't working, because I wasn't concentrating. Then I started wondering what kind of god makes you concentrate when your mother has just died and you've been up all night and all you're asking for is a little peace of mind, which if you had it, you could concentrate. When I started feeling like cussing, thinking *a little goddamn peace of mind is all I'm asking here*, I got up to leave. I blew out the candle, and the man crossed himself.

On my way out, I passed a sign that said, "Cathedral visitors are not to go about the church without a guide. Thank you." Though of course, there weren't any guides.

When I stepped outside, the sun had come up, which hurt my eyes. I didn't know how long I'd been in there, but it didn't seem like that long. The last of the darkness was vanishing, and the faithful were asking forgiveness for their sins and cleansing for their souls and receiving ashes on their foreheads, reminders of their mortality, as I walked back to the hotel, keeping my eyes lowered from the sun.

Carter was there, waiting, when I got back to the room. He'd showered and changed clothes.

"I'm glad you're here," I said.

He'd been worried about me.

I said, "What's going on up there?"

"Everything's taken care of." His voice was soft, gentle, a voice you'd use to tell children fairy tales.

He was holding me by now.

I was starting to let go of something, though I still hadn't cried. I got in bed and said, "Tell me I didn't kill her."

Tell me a story.

He got in beside me and said, "No. You kept her alive."

I curled myself into a hug.

"If it hadn't been for you," he said, "this would have happened a long time ago."

There was some truth to that. I believed I'd kept her from killing herself in the past, though I didn't know how Carter knew it.

"Your mother had a disease. You brought her more comfort in her last days than anybody else even tried to, but she was always in pain. Now she's not anymore."

That was true, too.

He was stroking my hair.

"In a way," he said, "she's better off."

Which was a bigger point than I wanted to argue.

It's just a thing people say.

I sat up. "I'm so tired," I said. "I shouldn't be tired. I should be doing something, making arrangements or calling people or something, but I'm so damn exhausted."

"You need your rest. There's nothing more to be done right now."

I lay back down. He pulled the covers up over my arms and kissed me on the cheek.

I should have saved the pill bottles. I knew that much already. I didn't even read the labels, which I also should have done. I knew that, too. But I had this irrational feeling that whatever I didn't know wouldn't be found out, so I didn't want to know anything more than I already knew.

I wasn't suicidal. That's the main thought that was going through my head during the three or four minutes it took me to destroy the key evidence: *I'm not going to kill myself.*

The rest of the evidence—my mother's body—my father destroyed.

Dr. Fontenot signed the death certificate in watery blue fountain pen ink, listing the cause of death as acute myocardial infarction—a heart attack—and Dr. Fontenot's brother, who had been appointed coroner two weeks before, didn't even ask for a toxicology report before my father had her cremated.

I PRESSED EJECT ON THE VCR AND TURNED off the TV.

I thought, *There are innocent ways to interpret my father having my mother cremated against her will.*

I was thinking of Huey Long—his hollowed-out biography, his grave on the front lawn of the Capitol, his body lying there inside it, rotting.

My mother was born in Algiers, across the river from New Orleans, though she wanted to be buried in New Orleans, where people have to be sealed into vaults because they won't stay underground. It's below sea level, so eventually it floods, and they float back up to the surface—or parts of them do, their bones. And as horrifying as it is to imagine your mother being cremated, I think it would be even more disturbing to worry about her skeleton not staying in her grave, her skull rising to the ground, being caught in the shovel blade of a grave digger.

I don't know why coffins with locks don't take care of the problem, unless the coffins eventually disintegrate. Maybe people rob them. Some people will steal anything they can get their hands on. And some people in New Orleans practice voodoo, which, even if you don't believe in it, you still don't want them using your mother's bones.

Cremation is not how people usually do things in southern Louisiana, but that's mostly because of Catholic tradition, and we're Episcopal, if anything. It's practical. My father is a practical man.

But then there's Huey.

Huey Long is buried on the front lawn of the Louisiana state capitol building where he was killed. Most people accept the official story, that he was shot by a disgruntled citizen, Dr. Carl Weiss, though some still argue that the single bullet responsible for killing Huey was a stray from overzealous bodyguards who shot Dr. Weiss at point-blank range, leaving sixty-two bullet holes in his body and a large number of scars in the granite wall against which he lay slumped when he died.

Every ten or fifteen years, somebody gets the brilliant idea of digging Huey up, presumably to prove once and for all how he died, though the bullet was removed at the time, so it's unclear to me what secrets might still lie in his coffin. But early during my father's tenure as governor, a professor from LSU tried to get permission to exhume the body. Knowing he'd get nowhere if he went through official channels, the professor went straight to the press, appealing to the people's "right to know," until one day he got his picture on the front page of the Baton Rouge *Advocate*.

That night, Huey's son, Russell, who hadn't spoken to my father for many years, ended a feud about which I had no knowledge—other than that it existed—to come to the Mansion and discuss the issue with my father. Trying to make him feel welcome, I brought him upstairs and served the two of them dessert in the private living room on the second floor.

I was coming in from the downstairs kitchen with a pot of coffee when I heard my father say, "You know, Russell, this whole problem could have been avoided if your uncle Earl had just followed his own advice when your daddy died." His mouth was full of food.

I stopped outside the door to listen. Earl Long was Huey's brother—also later a famously corrupt governor of Louisiana—and bad blood between Earl and Russell was part of the public record.

Russell said, "Okay, Governor, I'll bite. How so?" I couldn't see his face, but he sounded irritated.

"It's the same principle," my father said, and he quoted Earl Long's famous motto, " 'Don't write anything you can phone. Don't phone anything you can talk. Don't talk anything you can whisper. Don't whisper anything you can smile. Don't smile anything you can wink. And don't wink anything you can nod.' To that I'd add, don't nod anything you can bury, and don't bury anything you can cremate."

He laughed out loud, though Russell didn't. Russell thanked my father for the good advice, tactfully neglecting to mention that he'd once had that same Uncle Earl forcefully committed to an insane asylum.

I stepped into the room to see my father pick up the newspaper with its front-page photograph of the professor standing next to Huey's grave, tear it in half, crumple it back together, and toss it across the room toward a wastebasket. He missed, but Russell managed to say, "Good shot," without sounding sarcastic.

The next day, my father had a judge issue a restraining order against the professor. He was not to come within fifty feet of Huey's grave. Ever.

I WAS STILL STANDING IN FRONT OF THE TV, holding my mother's video in my hand, when I suddenly had that feeling where you can't remember why you've come into a room, as if your thoughts had been moving through the house separate from your body, and you've just come back together.

What am I doing here?

I was sweating. I pulled the sheets off the bed, carried them into the kitchen, and dropped them on the floor by the refrigerator. I closed the video back inside *Huey Long* and put it back in the box.

I looked around. The sheets and the walls were white, the box and the floor and the table were brown, the countertops were black. If my mother were there, she'd say, *What this house needs is color*—my mother loved color, believed in it the way other people believe in

God—so I opened the tool drawer and grabbed the pruning shears and went in the yard to cut flowers.

I pulled the honeysuckle off the fence so at least I could mask the smell of rot in the house until we got it fixed, though I had no idea how to do that, since once something's rotten, it's by definition past fixing. But I picked fire lilies and daisies and some furry things that I didn't know what they were called, and I cut magnolias as high as I could reach. I walked through the tall grass near the edge of the fence looking for wildflowers.

I thought, *I could lie down here and hide myself under a shroud of flowers and snip my wrists open and it wouldn't even hurt.*

It was a relief, sort of, the way knowing your seat cushion can be used as a flotation device is both comforting and terrifying.

I carried the flowers inside and lay them on the kitchen counter. I was feeling dizzy and hot, and I let my robe fall off so I was wearing just my nightgown, which was cooler. I knew I should keep busy— all the books on grieving say that—so I got out some beer mugs and started sorting through the flowers, separating them into piles, one pile for each mug.

My brain hurt and my chest hurt and I was feeling torn in half, and while I stuffed the flowers into the mugs, I kept thinking of that phrase "splitting headache" to reassure myself that other, sane people had felt what I was feeling and lived to tell about it. Then I filled the mugs with cool water—the flowers were already starting to die—and filled a glass of water for myself and swallowed two aspirin and dropped one aspirin into each mug.

I took the bed linens and my robe into the laundry nook and picked through the dirty clothes for things to throw in with the sheets.

I was trying to sort myself out as well. Part of me wanted to believe my mother. I wanted her not to have killed herself, wanted not to have let her kill herself. But a bigger part of me wanted to believe she was just talking crazy on the tape, the way I had been in the yard, feeling desperate and stuck where she was and trying to remind herself that life had a back door.

I switched the water temperature control to warm and turned the washing machine on to the normal cycle, which made me feel slightly better, turning dials, pointing arrows to WARM and NORMAL.

What I need is a hot shower. Or some coffee or a Xanax or a glass of wine or a good novel.

I knew I needed something, but I had no idea what.

I need to hide the video.

I went into the bathroom, closed and locked the door, stepped into the shower, and turned the water on. I'd forgotten to take off my nightgown—I was that distracted—and the fabric was sticking to my skin, which in that morbid mood made me think of a shroud, so I peeled it off, wadded it up, and dropped it into a corner of the shower. A big air bubble got caught in it and made it billow up like a child's ghost costume at Halloween, which bugged me like hell, so I stomped on it. The muddy footprint I left there was, for some reason, a relief.

I shaved my legs while I tried to come up with a plan of action. I needed some evidence, one way or another, before I did anything, but I had no idea where to find it.

I have to be clearheaded and persistent and linear, like a private investigator in a novel, though those have never been my best traits.

When I stepped out of the tub and looked in the mirror, it caught me up short, the sight of myself. I had my mother's watery blue eyes, which struck me as looking more like hers than mine somehow that day, and my face suddenly seemed old and tired and unfamiliar. I was thirty-five years old.

I don't exactly know who I thought I'd be by now, but I know I'm not that person.

I was starting to get a feeling like that professor must have had, a desperate sense of mission, like the truth must be out there some-where, buried, and it's up to me to dig it up and figure it out before it disintegrates. Though before that moment I'd always felt certain the professor must have been pathetically self-deluded, driven by dreams of grandeur and self-importance that would ultimately come to nothing.

A N HOUR LATER, I WENT TO THE BANK, filled out a safe-deposit-box form, and sat in a chair holding *Huey Long*, watching the blue door where the teller told me she'd come get me. I had an odd feeling, like I was on "Candid Camera," the TV show my mother and I used to watch together where things are never what they appear to be and all that really matters is whether you're able to laugh at yourself when you find out life has screwed you.

I said to myself, *No, Grayson, this is real*.

Eventually, the teller came to get me. She escorted me through the blue door, then two other locked doors, carrying a huge ring of keys like a jailer and not speaking to me. Something in me felt like screaming out, "I'm innocent," but I kept my mouth shut. I followed her into a square, windowless room, where she got out my box, handed me my key, and left. She closed the door behind her, slammed it so it made the same hollow sound prison doors do on TV.

My mouth tasted like dust. I looked around, trying to figure out how air got into the room. I was surrounded floor to ceiling by other people's safe-deposit boxes, and the walls around me were close and closing in, the boxes lined up row after row like the walls in the cemetery where they stack urns full of ashes. I was trying not to let myself hear the stories in those boxes, the letters and last words and last wishes locked away in them. I was feeling quietly terrified, as if my life had entered a place I'd never been before, a place I wasn't sure I'd be able to leave. I felt the air move around me, as if a page were turning.

When I started working, I worked quickly, slipping the book and the video into the box, and shivering. Then I locked the box and double-checked the lock, slid it back into its hole in the wall, and put the key in the zippered compartment of my purse.

The woman was waiting for me when I came out, tapping her foot like I'd taken too long, and I tried to pretend I was a plucky female detective. I thought about telling her a joke, but I couldn't think of one, and I figured she didn't have much of a sense of humor anyway. We were walking down the hall—I was following her again—and when we got to the last door, she opened it for me, and I very casually asked her if there was a way to find out whether my mother had a safe-deposit box.

Her eyebrow—just one of them—twitched.

"I know she did, actually," a lie, "but it's just that we can't find the key," another lie, obviously, and I couldn't tell if her expression was that she suspected me of lying or she was just a bitch, but I figured I'd gone that far, so I took a shot that she wouldn't recognize my mother's name—she probably wouldn't even know my father's—and I said, "Could you just verify that it was here, please? Instead of another branch? Her name was Marie Guillory."

She said, "Do you have her social security number?" which of course I didn't, so she wouldn't even look.

She fiddled with the button of her polyester pin-striped jacket, part of a fake power suit from the juniors department of a discount store, with a little smile. Her hair looked like a dead plant. I figured telling bank customers no was all the authority she had in this world, and a little self-knowledge might send her into a suicidal depression.

"Anything else?" she asked, benevolent now that she'd denied me something.

I needed to change my mailing address, and Carter had asked me to get signature cards next time I went to the bank so we could merge our checking accounts, but I didn't want to tell him I'd been there, and I suddenly didn't want a joint account. I didn't even want my bank statements to go to Carter's house. Up until that moment, I'd been perfectly happy to merge accounts, but now I just wanted my privacy, wanted to be able to spend money without anybody seeing what I'd spent it on. Carter made more than I did, and he didn't ask for accountings of my expenses, for what that was worth.

I said, "No, I'm fine. Thanks for your help," which came out sounding sarcastic, and walked out the door.

"Have a nice day," she said to my back, which echoed in my head like she'd said *have an ice day*. Which irritated me.

When I started my car, the air conditioner blew hot in my face, and I breathed it in deep and held it—a hangover from my aromatherapy phase. I was trying to figure out where to go next. The investigator in the novel I was reading would barge over to Dr. Fontenot's office and find out from him more graphic details than anybody would really want to know about what happens in an autopsy, why one wasn't done on my mother, and how he determined her cause of death. But she wouldn't care if my father found out she'd been asking questions, whereas I did, because no matter what I asked Dr. Fontenot, he'd tell my father I'd asked it. And whether my father was innocent or not, his instincts for secrecy in the face of an investigation would kick in, and he'd make sure I didn't find any information about anything from anybody.

So for lack of a better place to go, I went to a bookstore, and after a while, I was standing in the café with a stack of books and magazines, ordering a decaf iced cappuccino with skim milk, comfort food for dieters, and fumbling through my purse looking for my wallet while the cashier made it.

I paid and headed for the corner and passed the only other customer, a woman sitting alone at the center table, who was also drinking iced cappuccino. She held her mug up to me as if we had something real in common.

I smiled and nodded and looked away—*no, we don't*—and sat down. I tore a deposit slip out of my checkbook and put it on the table wrong side up, hoping a blank piece of paper would help me think straight, and looked up "rigor mortis" in *How to Solve a Murder*. The pages had been thumbed before. There was even a coffee stain on the rigor mortis page, which made me wonder how many people out there were secretly trying to solve murders, which made me wonder how many people out there are murderers, which made me think I was thinking too much.

"Rigor mortis," the book said, "begins about two hours after death, as the body chemistry slowly changes from alkaline to acid. The muscles, which were completely relaxed at death, begin to stiffen. The process usually appears first in the eyelids and the muscles of the face and then spreads to the jaw, the arms, the trunk, and the legs, in that order."

I wrote *2 hrs* at the top of my deposit slip, which wasn't technically blank. It had faint lines where you were supposed to write the amounts of the checks you were depositing. On the second line I wrote *eyelids*.

I had no idea what to do with that information.

I took a long drink of cappuccino.

I told myself, *Remain calm*—two words nobody ever says unless there's plenty of reason to panic.

My mother's eyes closed easily.

Things were happening fast and slow at the same time, the way it feels when your car spins out of control.

She'd probably been dead for less than two hours, which means that if I'd gone to check on her at midnight, when Carter and my father left to smoke cigars, she'd still be alive.

I wrote

face
jaw
arms
trunk
legs

A wave of something hot like regret washed over my face and tightened sour in my jaw, and by the time it got to my arms, it was as physical as nausea or cramps, but it was emotion, a cross between terror and despair and silent, screaming, paralyzing fury. I wanted to get up and get the hell out of there, but my stomach hurt so badly I couldn't stand up. My legs wouldn't move.

I could have saved her.

This was the thought I'd had probably a thousand times since she died, the thought I'd always tried to convince myself wasn't true, I did everything I could, and I'd reread the parts in my grieving books that said it was just survivor's guilt, a common though inaccurate feeling, but fuck that.

When did she die?

I tried to picture my father holding the hotel laundry bag before he put the pill bottles in it, tried to remember if it had been unfolded before, but I couldn't. I couldn't remember seeing him pick it up. I'd been lying there next to my mother with my eyes closed, blaming myself for her death, and at the time, I didn't think for even a second that if he'd finished off the job when he came in, suffocating her with a plastic bag, she might have died only moments before I walked in the room. It was unthinkable.

But three months later, the second I'd thought it, I tried to unthink it, and I couldn't.

I felt something rumbling in my gut, and I took a big swallow of cappuccino, which was supposed to be decaf but I felt it rushing through my blood while my brain was working in jerks, the world beating on and off like a heart, like a telltale heart, like a thousand flashbulbs going off inside me, exposing me.

I held my breath, trying to slow the rush.

I pictured a rose, a white rosebud lifting and opening, blossoming like in time-lapse photography. I exhaled and pictured a bird, a white seagull spreading its wings, dipping its beak in the rolling surf, a dove. I tried to imagine the sound of waves breaking on the sand, the earth gently breathing. I pictured the horizon at the ocean, the world quietly curving away out of sight, a boat sailing over the edge.

I counted my fingers. One two three four five. Six seven eight nine ten. I counted the heartbeats in my throat. One and two and three and four and five.

This is what I knew: My mother, who believed my father was trying to kill her, died sometime after midnight, more than likely of a lethal combination of prescription drugs—I didn't know which drugs—and vodka. There were no signs of struggle, either in the room or on her body. She had been both suicidally depressed and manically paranoid at times, though I wasn't aware that she was either when she died. She had long periods of mental health where she seemed happy, or at least unhappy in a not unhealthy way. I saw her the day she died, and she seemed peaceful, content—a state which sometimes follows the decision to commit suicide but which, of course, also occurs in people who are fine. She was on medication—antidepressants, lithium, Depakote, and Xanax. Maybe other things, too, maybe sleeping pills, I don't know. Both she and my father had easy access to those drugs. Though for that matter, so did

Dr. Fontenot. So did Carter. So did Luther, the butler, or anybody else on the staff. So did I.

I had no idea how long it took her to die and no way to find out without knowing when, what, and how much she took.

In a detective novel, this would be a perfectly plausible scenario for suicide.

It's more plausible for suicide than for murder because for one thing, how would the killer have gotten the pills down her throat? Unless he talked her into taking a sedative, injected her with whatever killed her or suffocated her after she fell asleep, and planted the empty pill bottles.

I didn't think my father knew how to give injections, but he could always learn. If heroin users can figure it out, it can't be that hard. Her nightgown had sleeves. And he would have known that nobody would check for needle marks.

If he suffocated her with the plastic bag I later threw away, there wouldn't have been any marks at all.

So there was my father's method and his opportunity, and they all had motives: My father obviously wanted to marry Audrey and did. He wanted to run for President, which is impossible to do in the age of TV if your wife is mentally ill. Audrey wanted to be First Lady. Dr. Fontenot could have ended up as Surgeon General. His brother may have been looking the other way just to keep his brother out of trouble, though maybe there was something else in it for him, too. I have no idea what a coroner's highest career ambition would be. Carter could and would have been anything my father asked him to. An ambassador, a cabinet member, Secretary of Something.

The woman at the other table said, "Excuse me."

I looked up. I'd been holding my head in my hands—I didn't mean to be that melodramatic—and I sat up straight, trying to act like nothing was wrong. The sun was behind her and I couldn't quite focus on her and she was still halfway across the café and I said, "Yes?" I said it softly, barely audibly: *Whatever you're about to say, you should come over here instead of screaming it across the room.*

She came closer, and she said, "I couldn't help but notice." She nodded at *How to Solve a Murder*, which I knew I should have covered with a magazine, *idiot me*. The thought occurred that she was following me, reporting back to my father, but she got here before I did, when nobody, not even I, had known I was on my way. I wasn't even going to entertain the ridiculous thought, which crossed my mind, that I was somehow being controlled. I knew I wasn't.

I said, "Oh, I was just . . ." I couldn't think of how to finish the sentence.

"Are you writing a murder mystery?"

She wasn't a spy. She was wearing a cat T-shirt and a big pewter cat necklace on a string and slightly too much blush. She reminded me of hot chocolate with marshmallows. She wanted my answer to be yes, and I couldn't think of a better one, so I said, "Actually, yes, sort of."

Then she was right at my table and I was afraid she was going to try to hug me—I don't hug strangers—but she stage-whispered, "I'm sort of writing a romance, but don't tell my husband. I always tell him I'm a hopeless romantic, and he says, 'Well, you got it half-right. You're hopeless.' "

She found this inordinately amusing.

I smiled and said, "Your secret's safe with me."

She winked at me and said, "So's yours."

Before she left, she invited me to her writers' club meeting—the first Tuesday night of every month, there in the bookstore. "It's mostly romance and murder mystery writers, so you'll fit right in, honey, although I guarantee, the minute a pretty little thing like you walks in the room, people are going to peg you for a romance writer."

She laughed again.

I smiled and said, "Thanks." She meant it as a compliment.

She said, "Bye-bye for now," and turned to go.

She left the book she'd been reading on her table. I would have expected a romance, but it was the memoir my father's only opponent in the re-election campaign, Michael King, had just self-published, a pack of lies.

I wanted to run after her and stop her, but what would I say?

I read the Baton Rouge *Advocate* while I finished my cappuccino, trying to put her out of my mind. Bay Summers, a former runner-up for Miss Louisiana who I'd thought had had an affair with my father, had been killed when a Nashville nightclub she was rehearsing in got bombed. They hadn't caught the bomber, but the only clue the police had, an anonymous call made from a pay phone, made them think they were looking for somebody who meant to bomb the gay bar down the street and got mixed up.

It stopped me cold. For a long while, I just sat there, staring at her picture, shivering and trying to hold the pixels on the paper together in my mind. I had chill bumps all over my body, which were feeling like pixels, like I wasn't completely connected in the spaces between them.

I was wondering what would have happened if Bay Summers had slept with my father and threatened to tell the media, thinking the exposure would help her career. She was younger than me by five years, not to mention prettier and much more ambitious. It wasn't hard to believe she was capable of cashing in on that kind of information if there were a market for it.

The question racing through me was, *What is my father capable of doing to keep that from happening?*

I wasn't blind to his faults. Given the right circumstances, he was capable of lying, cheating, two-timing, double-crossing, and breaking every promise he'd ever made, but he wasn't violent. In the worst of my parents' arguments, he never laid a hand on her.

He's a complex and ruthless man who's capable of just about anything, but he's not a killer. What happened is what seems to have happened, and whoever did this is just a fanatic, some idiotic, obsessive, manic-depressive paranoid fanatic who couldn't even find the target he was aiming for and who should have taken a Xanax and a bath and let whatever was bothering him take care of itself.

I closed my eyes and took a deep breath and let it out slowly.

I thought, *I should take my own advice,* but I'd left my Xanax at Carter's, and I didn't want to go back there until I was completely calm. I tried to make something black, like forgetfulness, or peace, wash over me.

Relax your eyelids, your face, your jaw. Your arms, your trunk, your legs.

It was far-fetched, the idea that my father had anything to do with Bay's death, a sign I was going overboard, which I tried to tell myself was a good thing—*Okay, Grayson, now you're being paranoid, which might be a sign that you're developing your mother's mental illness, but at least it means your father didn't kill your mother. On the other hand, if he didn't kill her, her mental illness, which you are now exhibiting symptoms of, did.*

I spent the rest of the day in the café, half of me trying to convince myself that I wasn't the murder-mystery equivalent of a hopeless romantic, and half of me trying to convince myself I was. I drank four cups of cappuccino and ate three croissants. I read *Time* and *People* and *The New Yorker* and all hundred and two pages of *How to Disappear Completely and Never Be Found.*

IT WAS LATE BY THE TIME I GOT HOME. Carter's car was already in the driveway. I had an urge to drive past the house and keep going until I ran out of gas, then hitchhike west until somebody killed me, but I pulled up behind him, got out of the car, and locked my doors.

I walked toward the house, carrying my keys in my left hand like I always did, but I felt strange. The house looked starker and colder than usual, which is how panic attacks start out—the world becomes angular and unfamiliar—though, I reminded myself, this time the house was different, all the flowers in the yard were gone.

Everything's fine, perfectly fine. One two three four five six seven eight keys on my key ring. And one in my purse for the safe-deposit box—nine. My apartment, Carter's house, my car ignition, my car door.

I couldn't think what the other four keys went to. I hadn't really noticed them before, couldn't remember when or how they'd gotten on my key ring, though I knew they'd been there awhile. I was afraid if I threw them away, I'd be locked out of some place I needed to go.

I unlocked the door and went inside. Carter wasn't in the kitchen, but the lights were on. I stepped into the living room where Carter always watched the news when he got home from work, but he wasn't there either. The fish were churning their water as if they hadn't been fed. I looked in his study, which was empty. I called for him and he didn't answer, which would usually bother me, not knowing where he was, but it didn't. It came as a relief from tension I hadn't even known I was feeling.

I went back in the kitchen and was pouring myself a glass of wine when it hit me, why I felt relieved—I didn't want to see him. I didn't want to see Carter or my father or Luther or Audrey or anybody I'd ever trusted again. I didn't even want to see my own face in a mirror.

The air conditioner clicked off. I hadn't realized it was on until it turned off, which was starting to become an odd little motif in my life, not understanding what was there until it was gone. In the silence, I heard a voice talking, though I wasn't hearing voices. It was a TV coming from our bedroom, and I had this panic—*what if Carter's watching the video?*—but of course he wasn't. He couldn't be. The video was at the bank, and the voice wasn't my mother's. It wasn't even a woman, it was a man's.

Calm down, Grayson.

So I walked down the hall toward the sound of the TV in our bedroom and stopped at the doorway.

Carter was stretched out on the bare mattress watching CNN and drinking a beer. He didn't look up, though I knew he could see me in his peripheral vision.

I said, "Hi."

It was an irritating habit he had, not looking at me when something was wrong.

He said, "Where are the sheets?"

Sheets?

I could have asked him what his problem was, why he wanted to know, because surely he didn't think I'd had another man in our bed, but I couldn't think of another reason anybody would be upset about sheets. Though I also didn't want to argue about what he thought I did all day because I didn't want to discuss what I actually did or what I'd been suspecting him of doing three months earlier.

"In the washing machine," I said, my voice even.

I was leaning against the door frame, trying to look like I didn't feel threatened or upset or furious or terrified or whatever it was I felt.

He said, "Why are you washing the sheets when you know the maids came two days ago?"

His voice was even, too. I couldn't tell what he was feeling, but whatever it was, he felt a need to hide it.

"What is this?" I said. "Am I going to get the third degree every time I do laundry?"

If he was mad and we were about to argue, I at least wanted some warning. He hadn't turned off the sound on the TV, so we weren't yelling, but we were talking louder than normal.

"I'm asking a question," he said.

There was a war on TV, a reporter standing in rubble, surrounded by thin, dead bodies, or maybe it was an earthquake.

I went to the bed and picked up the remote control and muted it, and Carter finally looked at me.

He said, "I thought you were going to move some more of your stuff."

"I was."

"But when I called here and you didn't answer, I called your apartment, and you didn't answer there all day. So I cut my afternoon short and came home early to see if you were okay, and you weren't here. You hadn't even unpacked your one box of books, so what, besides tearing apart the yard and turning this house into a funeral parlor, did you do all day?"

"I started doing a little housework, and I don't know why I washed the sheets. I just was sitting on them watching TV, and they seemed dirty. I didn't stop to analyze it. And then I was trying to make a centerpiece for the kitchen table, but I realized that all the flowers in the yard were planted by your ex-wife, and I suddenly started feeling like I was a guest in her house, so I wanted to get out of here for a while, and I didn't want to move more stuff in until I got over that feeling. So I went shopping because for one thing, the towels have her monograms on them, and every time I dry myself off, I think about you watching her dry her naked body off with the same goddamn towels. Okay?"

He turned off the TV.

I was still standing by the bed, halfway believing what I'd just said about what I'd done all day and trying to figure out why it was easier for me to lie to Carter than to a bank teller.

"I'm sorry," he said. "I was just worried about you."

He stood up to hug me.

I didn't want him to touch me, but I made myself lean toward him and hug him back.

I said, "You don't have to worry about me."

I am not my mother.

He said, "I didn't know that about the towels. I'm sorry, I just never look at them, never think about her."

"It's okay."

"Did you get new ones?"

"No. I wanted to look several places because they're so expensive, but the best ones were the first ones I saw, so I'll have to go back tomorrow."

He reached for his wallet. He was pulling out twenties.

"Get a whole new set, get two sets."

He put a stack of bills on my side of the dresser.

"Thanks, Carter."

I sat on the bed with him. He pulled me into his arms.

"I want you to be happy," he said.

I was feeling guilty.

I said, "I know."

"I'm sorry," he said, "I'm just really stressed out, which is no excuse, but I had a day like you wouldn't believe. The guy on death row told an Italian journalist that he's converted to Catholicism— he's got a Website and a whole Italian village behind him now—and I got home just wanting to see you and hold you, so when I saw the empty bed instead, it put me in a bad place."

"It's okay."

He once caught his ex-wife in their bed with a lawyer, a criminal lawyer. We bought a new bed, a new bedspread, but it was still the same room. We should have bought a new house.

He said, "I love you," though his voice sounded resigned to something other than, less than, what he really wanted.

Or tired. Maybe he was just tired.

I told him I loved him, too.

We lay there holding each other for a long time, not letting go. Eventually, Carter turned the TV on again and started skipping from channel to channel, interruption to interruption, which bugged me—whatever he was looking for, he wasn't going to find it—so I tried not to hear it. I was lying there, very still, with my hands resting on my stomach, looking at the ceiling.

Then I closed my eyes. In my mind's eye, I could see myself, laid out on the bed like a dead body.

After a while, I said, "Do you think it's the least bit possible that somebody killed my mother?"

Carter's body tensed up, though he didn't exactly move. He waited about two seconds longer than usual to answer me, a long two seconds while something in me was free-falling.

Then he turned to face me and I opened my eyes and looked at him. His forehead was full of worry wrinkles. His hairline was just starting to recede, and where his hair used to be, he didn't have wrinkles. He looked like he had two faces, one on top of the other, and one was too small.

He said, "Listen to me, Grayson." His voice sounded wrinkled as well. "Most people in mourning move from denial to fear to anger to bargaining with God to acceptance, but you accepted her death instantly—or you seemed like you did—but you've been moving backwards through the stages of grief ever since, and now you're in a form of denial."

I sat up.

"No I'm not."

He said, "Want me to be honest? I'm just trying to help."

I said, "Okay."

What else can I say?

"You're in a slightly paranoid form of denial."

Whatever was falling in me didn't exactly land, but it stopped falling. I didn't say anything.

How do you deny being in denial?

I looked toward the window and shook my head and something came out of my mouth that sounded like a one-syllable laugh, but it was just air. I didn't think anything was the least bit funny. There was music coming from the TV, people singing in harmony about cars.

"Don't flake out on me," he said.

"I'm not." I said it very carefully, pronouncing the final *T* with precision, like a witness in a courtroom.

"Don't do to me what your mother did to your father," he said.

"What is that supposed to mean?"

"Don't start turning yourself into your mother," he said.

"Don't bring my mother into this."

"You brought her up. You asked me if I thought she was *murdered*, for God's sake."

"I mean don't tell me I'm being like her. I didn't bring that up."

"Gray, don't do this. I didn't say you were like her, I told you *not* to be like her. I don't want to lose you, okay?"

Lose me? Is that some kind of threat?

I was shaking my head.

"Promise me?" he said.

I looked at the window. I was wondering how easy it would be for somebody to see in, wondering if somebody was watching us that very minute.

Maybe he's right, and I'm sounding paranoid, like my mother. Or maybe I'm starting to be paranoid about being paranoid.

He said, "Look in my eyes and promise me."

"Okay."

"Say you promise."

His voice sounded strained, desperate.

I wasn't entirely sure what I was promising other than to drop the subject, but I said, "I promise."

The only way I'm lying is if he's lying, in which case, my lying doesn't count.

He said, "Good."

And surely I would know by now if the man I've been sleeping with for the last three months had murdered my mother. I do know. He didn't. He's not that evil, and I'm not that stupid.

He lay down again.

The truth is, he's reacting exactly the way an exhausted but innocent person would react to someone he loved who had a genetic predisposition to bipolar disorder and was beginning to show signs of paranoia. So if that response bothers me, it says more about me than about him.

I put my head on his chest and listened to his heart.

He said, "Let's go to dinner and buy some towels."

"I'll make dinner. We don't have to get the towels tonight," I said.

But we did.

After, we came home and took a shower together and dried each other off. Carter combed the new-towel lint out of my hair during the ten-o'clock news.

I DIDN'T SLEEP THAT NIGHT. I LAY NEXT TO
Carter, playing the tape over and over in my head, analyzing every
nuance, coming to fifty different conclusions about what it meant.

Carter woke up once and asked me what was on my mind.

I said, "Nothing," which seemed like it bugged him, which
bugged me.

When he went back to sleep, I went into his study and snooped
through his desk. I didn't know what I was looking for, but I didn't
find it.

The next morning, I went to the Mansion. The parking lot was
packed, and a sign on the veranda read, *Welcome, Louisiana Archaeology
Society*. I used to fill in for my mother as often as I could at those functions, and every time an archaeologist told me how he was spending
his life constructing and reconstructing and deconstructing mean-
ings out of bone fragments and pottery shards, I started feeling des-

perate, as if everything meant nothing, and nothing mattered. I was starting to feel that way again, which should have been a comfort—for the past twenty-four hours, I'd been trying to convince myself that the video meant nothing, didn't matter—but it wasn't.

I tried not to take my feelings too seriously, though. I usually felt a vague sense of desperation there, which I usually ignored. A replica of a Louisiana plantation manor, the Mansion was built in 1963, at the height of the civil rights movement, by a governor who spent most of 1962 fighting court-ordered desegregation. All the staff are black because when they've tried to mix races before, it's created tension within the staff, and of course, none are free to leave. Given their other options, they're lucky to be in the house. So from one perspective, it's a highly effective rehabilitation program, but it also works uncomfortably like a replica of the whole slave system.

The policeman at the door ushered me through the vestibule into the foyer.

I waved to Luther, the head butler, across the room, but he was busy ladling out punch and didn't see me.

A woman with bleached hair and bleached teeth grabbed my hand and shook it hard and said, "Welcome to the Governor's Mansion. I'm Veronica Anderson, interim president, and you are?"

Her hands were rough and calloused with stubby nails. She'd spent a lot of time digging up dirt. She smiled, and her thick lipstick seemed about to crack, and I thought, *She should be selling coffins.*

I said, "Grayson Guillory, interim archaeologist."

She laughed as if I were a millionaire and she was a fund-raiser—everything's a food chain—and the man she'd been chatting up when I walked in took his chance to slip away.

Veronica motioned to the spot where he'd stood and said to me, "Professor Stradling and I—now where did he go?—we were just talking about how important it is to preserve our past before it disappears, and now *he's* disappeared."

She laughed again. I could see her placing a personals ad: *loves to laugh*.

When I heard the name Stradling, I recognized the face. He was the guy who tried to dig up Huey Long.

I said, "To tell you the truth, the more I know about Louisiana's past, the more I suspect that some or most of it might be better off disappearing."

Veronica's mouth sagged so fast I was afraid something had happened to her face-lift.

I wanted a glass of wine, but they weren't serving any that early in the day. Never put yourself in a room full of academics before four in the afternoon.

I looked at my watch and said, "Would you excuse me for just one minute?"

She said, "Of course."

I slipped into the kitchen and up the back stairs so she couldn't follow me—the second and third floors are the governor's private residence—and into my mother's bathroom, where I closed and locked the door. It was the first time I'd been up there since she died—every time Carter and I had come over, we'd stayed downstairs—and I leaned against the wall and closed my eyes. I was waiting—I'm not sure what for—but I was pulling myself open, wanting to be filled, and something inside me felt almost like it was praying. Then I started feeling dizzy and empty, like I was crying, though I wasn't.

I opened my eyes and counted the tiles on the floor under my feet, tried to let the numbers flow through my head like music. At first, they slid around in a kind of orderly chaos, like jazz, but before long they started marching through me like a high-school-pep-band headache, and I reached into my mother's medicine cabinet for some aspirin.

Though of course it wasn't there. All her things had been thrown out like trash and replaced by Audrey's makeup and wrinkle creams and nail polish and age-spot remover and estrogen patches and Retin-A—it was Audrey's bathroom now, Audrey's home—and I closed the mirrored door. The noise in my head wasn't music at all by then, just the dark, dissonant sound you hear before a symphony—fragments, musicians tuning their instruments, each listening only to himself—and I washed and dried my hands. Then I refolded the towel so it looked like I'd never been there.

When I came out of the bathroom I called for Audrey, thinking she might have been up there hiding from the archaeologists, but she didn't answer. So I went to my parents' bedroom and knocked on the door and called for her again.

"Audrey?" My voice sounded low and gravelly, like I was just waking up.

She didn't answer.

I put my hand on the doorknob, and a warning sounded in my head like an alarm and a shiver ran up my arm almost like an electric shock. It was the feeling—the certainty—that I was about to discover Audrey's dead body, and whoever killed her was going to kill me next.

I should get out of here now.

But I couldn't, not until I saw her for myself, so I turned the knob as quietly as I could, though it squeaked so loud I thought it had been booby-trapped, and I peeked in. And she wasn't there.

Of course she wasn't. I looked behind me. Nobody was lurking there with a knife in the air, waiting to kill me, too. Nobody was standing there at all, and I tried just to feel like an idiot, but I felt worse than that. I felt like a lunatic.

This is not normal. I'm worse than an archaeologist. I'm not even blowing trivia out of proportion, I'm breathing life into figments of my imagination, making ghosts. But I'm not crazy—not yet, anyway—because I still know what's real and what's not, and this is what's real: The room looks just like it always looks. The sun is shining. Everything is where it belongs. No dead bodies anywhere.

Which should have given me some relief, and which did, sort of, and didn't. So I tried to figure out what was wrong with the picture, and what I came up with was that nothing was different since my mother died, not one detail. The chair where she made the video sat where it had always sat, next to the same empty fireplace with the same antique duck decoys on the same hand-carved mantel. The same beige carpet and beige wallpaper, the same antique-reproduction four-poster bed, the same rose-covered Laura Ashley bedspread and pillow shams and striped bed ruffle, rows of rosebuds closed tight, like fists. Audrey and my father had made no attempt whatsoever to exorcize the ghost of my mother.

It's not how people act when they want to undo the past.

Which could have been a sign of innocence, like there was nothing they felt guilty about, so nothing to undo. Or a sign of guilt, like there was nothing they felt bad about because they wouldn't have undone my mother's death if they could have. Or a sign of heartlessness and utter complacency, like it hadn't occurred to them to change or not change my mother's bedroom because the only change that mattered to them was that she was gone. Or a sign of nothing. Two busy people who'd been married a month and who hadn't had time to take a honeymoon, much less redecorate.

I had to get out of there.

I could hear the murmur of archaeologists milling around downstairs—there was no more music in my head—so I went up the back staircase to the fourth floor, as far away from them as I could get. There was a rec room at the top of the stairs that previous governors' children or grandchildren had played in, but my father never used it, and the air was brittle and hard to breathe, like old cigarette smoke. I tiptoed past the big-screen TV, over the plaid carpet, and what was running in a circle through my head was, *Step on a crack, break your mother's back; step on a line, break your father's spine.*

I was trying not to listen to myself as I went into the attic area at the far end of the room and closed the door behind me. It was dark and hot and it smelled like dust, like memories disintegrating, history disappearing. When my eyes adjusted, I saw a bare bulb hanging from the ceiling and pulled the string, and the naked light fell over me, flooded the air and cast crisp, neat shadows.

The walls of one alcove were lined with Governor Edwards's gun racks, empty, of course, but he must have had a hundred rifles up there at one time and no telling what else—the ethics board was still looking for several hundred thousand dollars they thought he stole from the state—so I went in the other direction, climbing over an abandoned chrome dining room set and some bean bag chairs. I was headed around a corner when I almost tripped over a cedar chest. It was the chest my mother stored her pink suit in, a place she'd know I would look eventually, and I knelt down in front of it and placed my hands on it.

This is it. This is what I've been looking for.

I tried the lid, but it was locked.

I sat down on the floor in front of it. I briefly considered bashing it open with some kind of weapon or a baseball bat, but I didn't want to make that much noise. Then I looked at the hinges, trying to figure out how to break them, or whatever thieves do. I didn't know how to pick a lock. The thought ran through my mind that Luther might know—I didn't know exactly what his criminal past involved—but I figured the question would offend him, and whatever I found, if anything, I didn't want him to know I'd found it. I didn't want anybody to know I was looking.

I thought of my keys, the four keys I had that I didn't know what they were for—*maybe she left me the key*—and reached in my purse. I tried first one and the next and the next, and the last of the four keys slipped in, and I turned it. When the lock clicked, something clicked in my chest, and I opened the lid.

The suit from the inauguration was there, folded neatly, and next to it, the pale pink kid leather pumps she wore with it. I picked up the jacket and pressed it to my face. I could smell the cedar from the chest, but I just barely took in the scent of my mother as well, her perfume—lemons and evergreen and rain and just a hint of something earthy and angry, like brine. I folded it carefully and set it back on top of the matching skirt.

The only other things in the chest were a box and an envelope that a quick peek revealed held some old photographs. I saved the pictures for last, and I picked up the box. I was still sort of hoping for some kind of evidence one way or another—I didn't know what, since I knew if my father were planning to kill her, he wouldn't have put it in writing—but when I opened the box, there was nothing. It was full of makeup, my mother's makeup.

I picked up a jar of her foundation and unscrewed the lid. I touched my fingertip to it. It was wet and solid at the same time, and there was something about it that was forbidden and exhilarating, like touching her face—I couldn't remember ever touching my mother's face—and then I touched it to my own face. I rubbed the color of my mother's skin into mine.

I covered my whole face with it. All my little scars and blemishes and imperfections seemed to disappear. Then I put her eye shadow on my eyelids and her lipstick on my lips and her blush on my cheeks and I looked into her mirror. I wanted to see who she saw when she looked at herself. I wanted to feel what she felt, know what she knew, want what she wanted.

Then I picked up the envelope and pulled out the photos. Some school pictures of me that felt like images of a total stranger, a picture of our house in Hundred Oaks, a black-and-white photograph of my mother and Audrey wearing modest one-piece bathing suits and high heels, each with one foot just slightly in front of the other, their arms hooked around each other's waists. They looked so much alike, it was hard to tell who was who.

It was the day they met my father, the day history took the quiet turn that would eventually lead to my birth and, later, to my mother's death and my father's remarriage. Nobody involved had any idea of the consequences of their actions at the time. They had entered the Miss Louisiana pageant together—my mother won some cookware, a consolation prize, and Audrey won a two-hundred-dollar scholarship, which she never used, for placing in the top ten—and after the pageant, my father, who had helped build the set, introduced himself and asked Audrey to have dinner with him, but Audrey said no. She didn't date construction workers.

Six months later, my father married my mother.

Audrey eventually married a doctor and moved to Mississippi, but it didn't last, and she came back.

I wasn't trying to read meaning into a stack of old pictures. I hadn't gone through the bargaining-with-God phase of Carter's five-step grieving program, but I felt like I'd moved from one state of mind to another. I'd been sort of desperate, looking for clues everywhere, but I was pretty much ready to give up. I guess you could call that acceptance. So I wasn't hoping for anything when I slid my mother and Audrey to the back of the stack and found the next picture, a Polaroid of Dr. Fontenot in a bed, sleeping. He was nude, or at least his shirt was off. He had sheets pulled up to his waist.

Maybe I'd gone into denial again, because I thought, *Whatever story is behind this, I can't know it and don't want to imagine it.*

I moved to the next picture, an unaddressed, unmailed, unsigned postcard of a Mississippi beach with the words *be careful in N.O.* written on the back.

Whoever wrote this either sealed it in an envelope to mail it or, more likely, delivered it in person.

I didn't recognize the handwriting—it wasn't my mother's or my father's or Audrey's—and the next thing in the stack was a torn piece of yellow legal paper that had been folded and unfolded many times, and the same hand had written, *You are in danger*, and I knew I'd found what I'd been looking for. And already, I regretted having looked.

I was putting the photograph and the postcard and the warning together into one question while I went through the rest of the stack, and the next one was a strip of four black-and-white pictures, the kind people used to take in a tourist booth for a dollar, and they were all of my mother and Dr. Fontenot. My mother and Dr. Fontenot cheek to cheek, smiling, my mother and Dr. Fontenot, laughing, Dr. Fontenot looking at my mother, her head thrown back in abandon so the picture just showed her exposed neck. The last one was my mother and Dr. Fontenot, kissing.

A friendly kiss. Not necessarily more than that.

Years before, when my first marriage was falling apart, I'd had a brief affair with a married man. One day he started feeling guilty, but I thought I was in love with him, so I kissed him gently, a friendly kiss, and tried to argue we were just sharing some smiles and some laughs and some much-needed affection. I said we'd always be careful that nobody would find out so nobody would get hurt.

"Grayson, stop lying to yourself," he said. "This is not innocent."

I looked again at the strip of photographs, made myself look hard at what was there.

This is not innocent.

I moved on to the next photo, but it was me as a five-year-old, my first missing tooth. I was back to the beginning. Then I looked again in a panic at the kissing strip, but it was recent, or recent enough—within the last ten years—so at least I didn't have to worry that he was my father. I wasn't sure how I felt about my father or what I thought of him, but I knew I wanted him to be my real father.

I checked the envelope again. I didn't want to start putting together the obvious picture until I had all the available pieces, and there was one more thing, and I pulled it out. It was a letter. A typed letter that had been torn in half and crumpled. I could see my father wadding both halves into a ball and aiming it at a wastebasket across a room. Then it had been retrieved, probably by my mother, and taped back together and refolded to fit its original business-size envelope and folded over one more time to go in with the photographs.

I opened it quickly and read: *Dear Governor Guillory, It is with great regret that I offer my resignation from the position of Medical Adviser to the Governor. It has been a privilege serving you. I wish you and yours all good health. Respectfully, M. W. Fontenot, M.D.*

It was dated three years before, not long after the inauguration, and signed with the same watery blue fountain pen ink he'd used three years later to sign my mother's death certificate, the same ink the two cryptic notes were written in.

I lined it all up in front of me—the Polaroid of Dr. Fontenot in the bed, the *be careful* postcard, the *you are in danger* note on yellow legal paper, the strip of photographs, the resignation.

Then I picked it all up and sort of shuffled everything around and put them down again: the resignation, *be careful*, the strip of photographs, *you are in danger*, the bed.

And again: the bed, the strip, *he knows, be careful*, the resignation.

I wanted to put them in chronological order, but the only thing that was dated was the letter.

This is what's here: My mother and Dr. Fontenot had an affair, probably during the campaign, when my father was on the road most of the time and my mother claimed to be too nervous to travel. Soon after the inauguration, Dr. Fontenot offered his resignation, but my father didn't accept it. At some point, maybe before he tried to resign, maybe just before my mother died, something happened—maybe my father found out about the affair, or maybe something else entirely—and Dr. Fontenot felt my mother was in danger, so he tried to warn her.

Half my brain was trying to come to terms with that much while the other half was spinning elaborate conspiracy theories: *What if my father was blackmailing Dr. Fontenot, making him warn her because he wanted her to think she was in danger even though she wasn't so she'd seem paranoid and therefore dismissible, or so she wouldn't say anything about his affair with Audrey, or so she'd give him a quiet divorce, or so she'd confront him about the danger and he could tell her she was insane, which, if she believed him, would depress her, and she'd put her guilt about her affair and her anger about his affair together with the belief that she was going insane and kill herself?*

It was possible—it was within the realm of possibilities—but it didn't help.

Okay, so there's a way to stretch it where it doesn't prove my father's guilt, but there's no way in hell to make it prove his innocence.

I tried to think how a normal person would handle the situation, but a normal person would call the police, and I couldn't do that. State police guard the Mansion twenty-four hours a day and there weren't words on the planet that would make any one of them accuse my father of murder. For one thing, they wouldn't believe it—they got where they were partly because of their blind loyalty to him. For another thing, what would happen to a cop's career after he accused the governor of murder? What would happen to his life? I didn't know—I didn't think it had ever been done—but it couldn't be good. There was no evidence—undated, unsigned, unaddressed, and unmailed cryptic little messages wouldn't count for much in the legal world, and if there ever was anything that would hold up in court, I destroyed it the night she died. I had a chance to keep it, hide it, study it, even turn it over to the police, but my father handed it to me, trusted me with it, co-opted my suspicions before they'd even begun to form. All he said was, "Take care of this." And I destroyed it.

Which wouldn't keep the media from finding out if I called the police, and they don't need evidence to crucify a politician or anybody near him once they have an accuser, for which my father and Carter and Audrey would never forgive me. So with one phone call, before one piece of evidence had been produced, I'd destroy all the family I had left.

And it still wouldn't bring back my mother. Justice still wouldn't be done. The sheriff was an old friend and hunting buddy of my father's for whom my father had had three domestic violence charges—and God only knew what else—thrown out, and he'd just refuse to arrest him. No district attorney in this state would prosecute him, and no judge, most of whom were appointed by him, would convict him, which could have sounded like a paranoid conspiracy theory on my part, but it wasn't. Nobody conspired because nobody had to. Everybody in Louisiana politics knew, independently, not to cross my father, and nobody did. And if, improbably, there were an honest judge or DA and the case miraculously got that far, it simply would not be assigned to him.

I was suddenly very tired and hot and uncomfortable, and I felt like a fool. I wanted to get out of there.

I thought about taking the letter and the photographs with me, but I figured they were safer locked in the attic. Obviously, nobody knew they were there, or they would have been destroyed like everything else. So I put them back in the chest.

I closed the lid, and I was about to lock it when I opened it again. I picked up her jacket to take in one last breath of her.

Then, for no reason, I unfolded her skirt, and a handgun fell out. A tiny pistol the size of a fist, which I felt like a punch in my gut. *You could fit this in an evening bag, hide it in a pair of shoes.*

It didn't make sense.

You could kill somebody with it.

My mother didn't want to kill anybody.

One, she didn't know how to shoot a gun. Two, she didn't want to know. She hated guns. And three, even in her worst paranoid fantasies, she didn't need one. Even if somebody was trying to kill her, nobody was trying to shoot her. So she wouldn't have bought it for herself. And if my father were trying to kill her, he wouldn't have bought it for her.

I had pretty much ruled out the theory that he was trying to get her to commit suicide, but even if he were, anybody who knew my mother would know that if she had killed herself, she wouldn't have used a gun.

But if you're the governor's wife and for whatever reason you decide you want a gun and you don't want your husband to know you have it, you can't just get one on the street. Somebody had to give it to her.

I picked it up. It was heavy for its size. It was real.

You are in danger.

I turned it over in my hand. I didn't know much about guns, but I could see it was an automatic, not a revolver. I didn't know how to tell if it was loaded.

Fontenot.

Dr. Fontenot was an avid hunter and gun collector. It was not hard to believe that he would have wanted anybody he loved to carry a weapon.

Another reason their affair doesn't make sense. Another reason nothing does: If he loved her enough to give her a gun, he wouldn't have killed her.

I didn't want the gun, but I didn't want to leave it there. I closed my hand around the grip, which felt solid and substantial. My body felt like it was disintegrating into air.

I slipped my finger easily into the trigger. Then I touched the barrel to my tongue. It was cold and tasted bitter. I closed my eyes.

I don't know what I was doing. But it seemed to release something in me. After a minute, I took the gun out of my mouth.

I'm not going to kill myself. No matter what happens, I will not kill myself.

I had had this thought before, but it seemed like a revelation this time.

I was sweating, but I felt calm, focused in a way I hadn't been before.

I still didn't want the gun, but I put it in my purse. I folded her jacket and her skirt and put them back in the chest.

Then I picked up her shoes, which I wanted for reasons I didn't fully understand other than I just wanted something.

WHEN I WENT DOWNSTAIRS AGAIN, THE archaeologists were gone, and Luther was in the kitchen polishing silver. A pot of coffee was brewing.

I went in and put the shoes and my purse with the pistol in it on the counter and said, "Hi, Luther."

He acted like he didn't notice the shoes.

"Miss Grayson Guillory herself," he said, smiling, his teeth bright against his skin. "I thought you'd forgotten all about me."

I made myself smile apologetically.

He said, "I know you've been busy."

I said, "Oh, things are crazy," an expression I don't usually use and instantly regretted, but I didn't know how to take it back. My mother's makeup was all over my face, her affair with Dr. Fontenot was in my head, and her shoes and her gun were on the counter. Nothing was where it was supposed to be.

Luther got out a cup and saucer—just one—and said, "Coffee?"

He was standing straight with his legs together, and the tone of his voice was stiff and polite, what he'd use with a stranger.

I said, "Thank you."

He offered to pour my cream.

I said, "Thanks, but I'll do it."

He set the pitcher down without saying anything, though he seemed just slightly offended. He was acting like a butler, which was his job, but he didn't have to act that way around me—we were friends—and he knew it. Or he should have known it, unless we weren't really friends, in which case, I needed to know that.

I said, "Aren't you having any?"

He said, "No."

Then the house was loud with quiet.

I said, "I'm sorry I haven't been around. I'm moving in with Carter—actually, we're getting married—so all my stuff is in boxes and I'm sort of at loose ends."

"Whoa. Back up," Luther said. "You're getting married?"

"Yeah."

"To Carter?"

Of course to Carter.

I nodded.

"When?" he said.

"We're not sure yet."

Say you're happy for me.

Then something happened inside him, a slight shift in thinking. He was back to playing his role, the male girlfriend, though I'd never been particularly conscious of it as a role before.

He said, "If I ask you where it will be, are you going to tell me it's here so I can come, or you going to break my heart?"

I said, "Okay, we'll have it here."

"Well, this calls for a toast," he said.

He poured himself a cup of coffee and held it up.

"To your happiness," he said. "Richly deserved."

We drank and smiled at each other, trying to find something that was lost. We used to sit around the kitchen every morning drinking coffee, chatting like housewives while my mother slept upstairs, and part of what used to connect us was the fact that we were her caregivers, together. But one way or another, we'd failed at keeping her safe, and our failure sat between us like a dead body in the room, still and silent and impossible to ignore but impossible to address.

I couldn't ask him why he wasn't saying he was happy for me.

But I am, he would say. *Of course I'm happy for you.*

And I couldn't ask him about the gun. I didn't want anybody to know I'd found it.

And I didn't want to ask him about the part in the video where my mother said the butler was giving her drugged coffee, but I felt like I had to.

I said, "I was just wondering, did Dr. Fontenot ever . . ."

Luther just barely shook his head and went back to leisurely polishing silver. Whatever I was about to ask, he didn't want me to ask it.

"Did he try to advise you about taking care of my mother?"

It stopped him up short. He put the teapot down.

I said, "For example, did he ever give you medicine to give her?"

"No," he said, his voice turning into a question. He picked up the teapot with a jerk, as if he were trying to undo having put it down. Then he rubbed a spot of tarnish.

I said, "Did she ever refuse to take her medication?"

"Not that I know of."

I said, "I was just wondering." I shrugged.

The teapot was as tarnish-free as it had ever been, but he was rubbing it like a magic lamp. I wondered what he was wishing for, what he knew, what he wanted to know or wished he didn't know. I didn't know what I wished either, but I ached with wanting whatever it was.

Luther said, "You all right?" He almost whispered it.

"I'm fine," I said.

A pause, then, "You just need some rest."

It's what he used to say about my mother when she was so depressed she couldn't get out of bed.

She just needs some rest.

Something about the way he was acting scared me and touched me and made me mad, all at the same time. I felt like laughing and crying. I felt very old and very young. I felt fragile and indestructible and unfamiliar to myself.

I am not crazy.

I said, "What, Luther?"

He said, "What?" He looked at me with his eyebrows slightly furrowed.

I couldn't tell if he was worried about me or my line of questioning or something else, but I didn't know how to do what I needed to do discreetly, not at that moment, so I said, "Tell me what you're not saying."

He was rinsing the teapot.

I said, "Please. I need to know."

I waited until the pot was clean. Some part of my head was rambling on quietly about watched pots, while another part was trying to keep from screaming.

Then he turned to me and said, "You be careful."

You are in danger, be careful.

The house fell silent again. Somewhere, somebody had been doing something that was making white noise like static—vacuuming or blowing leaves outside, maybe—but they stopped. I suddenly had a feeling that someone was listening, and Luther seemed to have the same feeling. He looked away from me toward the sink, turned his back to me to end the conversation. He dried the teapot with a towel, taking care not to touch it with his bare hands.

I picked up the shoes and my purse.

"Okay," I said. "I guess I better be going."

"You get some rest now."

I WENT STRAIGHT TO THE CAPITOL FROM
the Mansion. In the car, I counted my thoughts on my fingers.

1. *Luther is not in on it.*
2. *There is no "it."*
3. *Luther would never try to make me think I was crazy.*
4. *If anybody were trying to make anybody think they were crazy,
   they'd do more than tell them to be careful and get some rest.*
5. *Dr. Fontenot's note could have been meant for someone else, anyone
   else. It could have been about something totally unrelated to my
   father. Who doesn't need to be careful? Especially in New Orleans?*
6. *It could have been meant for me—why else would I have been given
   the key to the chest?*
7. *Nobody who was conspiring anything would give her a gun or leave*

it in the chest. It was just there because it was hers. It was her secret, and she had no place else to keep her secrets. She had no privacy.

8. *The photographs of my mother with Dr. Fontenot prove nothing. They prove that he loved her. He found her beautiful, he wanted to protect her, and he loved the sound of her laughter. She knew he did, and it made her happy, and assuming she's the person who left the key to the chest on my key ring, she wanted me to know it, too.*

I wanted just to be glad for that, to know that she'd had a moment of pure joy and leave it at that.

But of course I couldn't. For one thing, why didn't she mention Dr. Fontenot's warnings in the video—surely if they had anything to do with her suspicions, she would have—so I tried to put the kiss and the warnings together with the image of Dr. Fontenot in his white tie and tails standing over my mother's body the night she died, crossing himself, praying for her soul, when it occurred to me that either he was involved in the murder, supplying both the drugs and the cover-up, or there was no murder.

If he loved her enough to warn her when he thought she was in danger, to supply her with a gun, then he wouldn't have also conspired with my father to kill her. But my father couldn't have done it and wouldn't have gotten away with it without Dr. Fontenot's help, which proved he didn't do it.

I was suddenly feeling much better.

I put the gun under my seat, got out of the car, and walked up the steps to the Capitol building—forty-eight stairs, one for each state in the Union when the Capitol was built, with Alaska and Hawaii commemorated later on the plaza. I went inside through the metal detectors and got in the elevator, going up, and something inside me was rising as well, but when I passed my father's floor, it stopped. The elevator stopped, and the doors opened, but nobody got on.

Maybe he didn't kill her, but he didn't love her. He drove her to the arms of another man. Then he drove her to suicide, which, in a way, is worse than killing her.

The doors closed, and I kept going.

When I came to Carter's floor, the elevator stopped again and the doors opened again, but I still didn't get off. I let the doors slide closed, and I kept going up until I came to my godmother's floor and stepped off. My godmother, Laura Cormier, was the lieutenant governor, and when I walked into her outer office, her secretary, Jolie, looked up from her computer screen and said, "Grayson! Long time no see!"

Then her face froze—she remembered why I hadn't been around for the past three months—and then she tilted her head and turned her face into a sad-puppy pout and said, "How've you been?"

"Fine," I said.

"I'm just so glad to hear that, sweetheart. I've been thinking about you."

A half-dead rose slumped in a bud vase on her desk, and the wall behind her was plastered with greeting cards and cartoon rainbows and Bible verses printed on floral watercolor backgrounds and a huge photograph of a beach with the legend of the footprints printed over it—the one about Jesus carrying you through the hard times. It was overkill, in my opinion, that suggested a quiet desperation. Though I might have been projecting my own feelings onto her.

"Thanks," I said.

"You look terrific," she said, but the way she emphasized look made me think she was assuming I was a wreck inside.

"Is Laura in?" I said.

"You know what, sweetie? She's in a meeting, but she'll be back just real, real soon. I thought she would have been back by now, so I'm sure she won't be long. You want to wait in her office?"

I wanted to get out of there, but I didn't want to go back through the lobby downstairs yet because I didn't want the gossips at the information desks to mention to Carter or my father that I was here for two and a half minutes because I didn't want to have to explain to either of them what I'd been doing there—I didn't exactly *know* what I was doing there—and all the other exits set off alarms. But I didn't want to stay there with Jolie because I didn't want to be called sweetie again, though I knew she didn't mean anything by it—she probably called the trusties sweetie, too. It was probably some defect in my character, but I didn't want to be the recipient of any more of her kindness. It made me feel indebted and ungrateful and sticky, so I went into Laura's office and closed the door.

I figured Jolie was out there praying for me while she typed.

The Yellow Pages were sitting on the credenza behind Laura's desk, and I looked up Detective Agencies, for the hell of it. It was just before Detectors—Metal & Treasure. I tore out the page and called the one with the biggest ad—he handled divorce, child custody, and missing persons with complete confidentiality—but I got a recording, the number had been disconnected, and I hung up. You don't have to have any qualifications to be a PI, just enough money to rent an office, and this guy apparently ran out of that.

I tried another one, the second-biggest ad. There was no mention of confidentiality with this one, but the results were guaranteed, whatever that meant.

What the ads don't say is that they don't know and don't try to find out who's the better spouse, the better parent, the better home for the person who ran away. They're just trying to make a buck, pay the phone bill, so once they gather incriminating information, why not sell it to the highest bidder? It beats going out of business.

I figured most people who would accept money to violate somebody else's privacy, like most people who would pay them money to do it, aren't overburdened by scruples in the first place.

I got his machine and hung up.

How discreet could he be if he expected you to leave proof that you'd called him before you even hired him?

I tried one more, just a name and a phone number, thinking maybe he's too cheap to buy an ad, but maybe he's so good he doesn't need to advertise. When he answered the phone, he said his name, so I figured it was him, not a secretary or assistant. I said, "I know somebody you're working for, and I'm willing to pay double whatever she's paying you if you tell her you found nothing and turn your results over to me."

There was a long silence on the other end.

I said, "Triple."

Silence.

"Triple plus fifty thousand dollars."

"Who is this?"

I hung up. Less than fifteen seconds. That's how long it would take him to sell me out. I put the page through Laura's shredder.

Even if nothing my mother suspected turned out to be true, the fact that I was having my father investigated to prove it wasn't would be big news, and if a PI sold out to the highest bidder, I couldn't begin to outbid the newspapers for my own story.

I closed the phone book. The end.

I picked up the phone and dialed my mother's doctor's office. I knew the number by heart, and I recognized the receptionist's voice when she answered—Stephanie. I was afraid she'd recognize me, which was an irrational fear, I realized even then, because she'd find out who I was eventually if I went in, but when I asked if there was any way she could fit me in for an appointment that afternoon, my voice came out so high and girlish that I didn't even recognize it.

Stephanie said, "Are you a new patient?"

I said, "Yes," which felt heavy in my throat, like a lie, though it wasn't. I'd never been to any kind of psychiatrist or psychologist.

She said, "Dr. Mornay doesn't have any new patient appointments available for six weeks."

How many people who need to see a psychiatrist can afford to wait six weeks?

"But my mother was a patient of his, and I need to talk to him."

"Would you like an appointment in six weeks?"

"Okay."

"Your name?"

I didn't want to give her my name.

I said, "I'd rather keep my privacy, if that's okay." I was feeling stressed out and vulnerable, and I was doing the best I could.

"I can't make an appointment without a name, but don't worry. We don't give this information out to anybody. Nothing said or done in our offices ever leaves these walls." Her voice was soothing, almost musical.

She's used to dealing with crazy people, and she thinks I'm crazy.

"Even to family members, like if somebody wanted to know something about their family member?"

"No."

"Even after their family member died, and they just wanted to know what happened? They just have some questions?"

"Not without the patient's written consent or a court order, nothing is revealed to anybody for any reason."

"Oh. Well, okay."

"So, your name?"

"Never mind."

I hung up the phone.

My heart was pounding, and I sat down in the leather chair in front of Laura's desk and crossed my legs. I arched my foot and tried to relax.

There was nothing more I could do. Maybe he killed her, maybe she killed herself. How much difference did it really make?

Once, my parents were arguing loud on the deck outside my window at a rented beach house. I was in bed, supposed to be asleep, when I heard something shatter like gunshot and they went completely silent. I thought one of them had killed the other. I thought my father had killed my mother. I'd been curled up in a ball, listening to them fight and shivering, but when I heard the noise, I stretched out flat with my arms beside me, very still, and pretended I was Barbie. I was beautiful and plastic and I didn't have parents and my feet were arched in permanent but invisible high heels.

The next day, I didn't ask them about the argument or the noise and they didn't mention it. We all just pretended it had never happened.

I arched my foot toward Laura's desk like Barbie's until my shoe slipped off. I tried to pretend I was plastic.

I never knew what the argument had been about, but remembering it there in Laura's office, I had to wonder if it was Dr. Fontenot. I had no idea when that whole thing started or when or why or how it stopped, but I was starting to feel like my whole childhood had been an illusion.

I could feel the sun warming my plastic hair on my shoulders, and I turned my plastic neck to look out Laura's window, but we were too high up—there was nothing to see but sky—so I looked at her painting. It was a dog running through marsh grass with a dead duck in its mouth.

I started to calm down. Soon, I couldn't even feel my heart.

Then I just sat there for a while waiting on Laura, trying not to think about my mother, trying not to think at all.

I'll tell her I'm planning the wedding and I wondered if she wanted to come dress shopping with me.

We hadn't set a date, had barely discussed what kind of ceremony we wanted. Part of the problem was that Carter was from a big family, Catholic, and divorced, though of course there were other unresolved issues as well.

My little epiphany about Dr. Fontenot loving my mother was wearing off. Maybe he loved her, for at least a moment, but people fall out of love. Once, I was in love with Ray, or I thought I was, which is the same thing. Carter used to be in love with his ex-wife. For all I knew, my father had been in love with my mother at some point.

When Laura came in, she said, "Hi," and I said, "I need your help."

I meant to sound casual—I should have stood up to give her a little Junior Leaguer hug and asked her what Barbie would have worn to her second dream wedding if things hadn't worked out with Ken—but it came out sounding scared and desperate, which made me feel desperate, and all of a sudden I was holding my breath to keep something from collapsing inside me.

She closed the door behind her and asked me very gently if I wanted some coffee, and I shook my head no.

She said, "Water? Coke?"

No.

"Valium?"

I said, "Don't make me laugh or I'll cry."

"You can cry if you want," she said. "Sometimes you need to let it all out." Her first husband died of pancreatic cancer, and she thought she knew what I was going through.

"Thanks," I said, "but I don't want to."

I was holding tight to the arms of my chair, and she sat down in the chair next to me. We were both facing her desk and, behind it, diplomas and certificates of appreciation and pictures of Laura and her second husband with their arms around her kids, Laura shaking hands with three different presidents, Laura with my father, his arm around her waist.

She massaged my hand and my wrist, the way my dentist's assistant used to while he drilled holes in my teeth.

"You're afraid if you start, you'll never stop?"

That wasn't exactly it, but I nodded so hard it hurt my teeth.

She said, "But you will. I think the hardest times for me were about three months after, when all the flowers and casseroles had been acknowledged and the sympathy cards had stopped coming in and the death as an event was over, but I wasn't anywhere near over it, and then again when I decided to get remarried, because I felt guilty, and I felt angry at the guilt, because after all the pain, something good was finally happening and I couldn't fully enjoy it. And you're in both of those places at once right now, plus, you're moving, so you're under enormous stress. You're off the charts. But I promise, it will ease up. You'll even laugh again without feeling like you're going to cry at the same time."

I knew she was trying to help, so I didn't interrupt her, but that was page one of every grieving book there is, and I didn't want to hear it.

I said, "Ever since my mother died, I'm feeling confused."

"Of course you are," she said. "That's very normal. What are you confused about?"

I was trying to make myself ask her about wedding dresses and flowers and food, mother things, but I said, "Sometimes I think somebody killed her."

She didn't flinch.

She said, "Any idea who?"

"My father."

She glanced around the room. I didn't know if she just didn't want to look at me because she thought I was nuts, or if she was trying to take in what I said because she thought it sounded true, or if the same thought had just occurred to her that just occurred to me, that her office might be bugged, but she said, "Let's go for a walk."

We took the elevator down. We were alone at first, but we didn't say anything. We were both waiting until we got out of the building. On the fifteenth floor, a trusty wearing an orange jumpsuit and rolling a huge trash can on wheels got in with us and asked how we were doing. We smiled and Laura told him we were fine. The elevator doors closed, and we all nodded our heads. Yep, fine.

The Mansion is the only place where all the trusties have committed the same crime. That janitor could have been a drug dealer, a kidnapper, a car thief, a bank robber, a wife beater—just about anything but a sex offender or a serial killer. I was looking at him, trying to figure out what he'd done, but he just looked normal, like he'd never done much of anything. He got off on the fourteenth floor, which is really the thirteenth, and told us to have a nice day.

Laura said, "You too," and we went on to the lobby in silence.

The lobby was full of children, a school group of wiggly fourth-graders taking a tour, none of whom was listening to the guide tell them how many different kinds of marble Huey Long brought in from all over the world to build the place.

We waited for them to move out of our way, toward the hall where Huey was shot. Then we went out the front door and headed down the steps.

We still weren't saying anything. I was barely even thinking anything, just the names of the states that were carved into the stairs—Arizona, New Mexico, Oklahoma, Utah—wishing I were anywhere but where I was.

When we got to the bottom—Connecticut—we crossed the street to walk in the garden on the front lawn.

I was waiting for Laura to ask me why I thought what I thought, and I was wondering what I'd say, whether I'd tell her about the video or the stuff in the attic or the affair with Dr. Fontenot, how sure and how reasonable I'd sound, but she said, "Grayson, you need to think long and hard about what you're doing and what good could possibly come from doing it."

We'd skipped a step, it seemed to me, and my heart sort of skipped a beat, it felt like.

One, she has no idea what I'm doing.

There was no way for her to know about the video, and everything else I was doing stemmed from there.

Two, unless she knows everything.

Unless she knew more than I did about what I was doing because regardless of whether she knew where I'd started, she knew where I'd finish. She knew what I'd learn if my questions ever got answered.

We walked toward Huey's grave in the center of the yard, where there was a bench facing the Capitol. When we sat down, I said, "I'm not doing anything."

She didn't respond.

I said, "What do you think I'm doing?"

"Don't be naive, Grayson. You're informing the lieutenant governor that you suspect the governor of murder, and what I assume you're about to tell me is that you have no evidence whatsoever and that in a moment of extreme emotion you misstated your position, which is, like most children of suicides, you blame the other parent, who you feel is morally but not legally and not literally responsible for the death."

It could have been true, what she was saying. It sounded reasonable.

I didn't answer her right away. I just stared at Huey's tombstone. It's a huge marble column with a model of the Capitol building on top of it and a statue of Huey, twice as tall as the Capitol, resting his hand on the top floor, like a god. The god of Louisiana politics. In which case, I thought, God help us all.

Laura had obviously been told it was suicide, not a heart attack, where I'd assumed that Carter, my father, Dr. Fontenot, his brother the coroner, and I had an unspoken agreement not to tell anybody, but I didn't know what to do with that information.

A yellow bus full of children pulled up in front of the Capitol.

"As an officer of the state," Laura said, "I'm responsible for any information you give me."

It was a Catholic girls' school. They began filing out of the bus, and they were all dressed identically, in white short-sleeved blouses and plaid kilts. They were all black, and they looked like they were all about nine years old. Most children start running up and down the stairs at this point, screaming, but these instantly formed a straight, quiet line on the sidewalk behind the nun. I wondered what she threatened them with to make them shut up. Excommunication, probably. Hell. Carter still had nun nightmares.

"I'm sorry," I said. "I didn't come to you as lieutenant governor, I came to you as a friend. I just wanted to talk."

Laura didn't move, and she wouldn't, until I said what she needed to hear.

Okay, fine.

"And no," I said, "I don't have any proof."

She still didn't move.

"I'm sorry," I said, "but I just have all these suspicions and doubts and things that don't add up that I need to talk to somebody about, but who am I supposed to talk to? Maybe the whole thing is all in my head, but I can't go to a psychiatrist. For one thing, I don't know who's on what side, who would use my suspicions to try to destroy my father, or who would use them to destroy me. I know that sounds paranoid, and maybe it is, but if he's capable of murdering his own wife, then it's not out of the question. So for that reason, not to mention what my mother went through, I wouldn't trust a psychiatrist with my laundry, much less my brain."

Laura said, "You don't need a psychiatrist."

"I know I don't. Which is why I'm here."

I waited.

After a pause, she said, "How are things with Carter?"

Carter?

I didn't know if she was playing therapist, trying to help me, or being her own private investigator, questioning me.

"Carter's fine."

For all you know, Carter has nothing to do with this, so what's your question?

"Can't you talk to him?"

"Yes. But not about this."

"Why not?"

"Because I love Carter, but I also believe he would do anything for my father, including tell him my secrets. I know how that sounds, and I hope to God I'm wrong, but I'm sorry, sometimes it's what I think. Or it's what I fear, what I try not to think. But I also know my father, and if he is behind something like this, he's already found a way to keep his hands clean and implicate somebody else, namely Carter, because Carter's his alibi, the only person who was with my father the whole night she died. So they're either both innocent or they're both guilty, and if they're guilty, and if somebody pays for what they've done, it will more than likely be Carter, while my father walks. And if that happens, I don't want Carter or me to have to look back and think it's my fault that he's spending the rest of his life in jail."

Laura said, "Nobody's going to jail."

Which is probably true, though not the same thing as saying nobody's guilty.

"But okay, hypothetically," she said, "why would it be your fault if Carter went to jail for something he did of his own free will?"

"Because without me, he would have gotten away with it. You know that Carter told the press it was a heart attack when he knew it wasn't true, don't you?"

"Yes," Laura said. "Can I be blunt?"

"Yes."

"You're as guilty of that cover-up as he is. We all are."

"Who is 'we'?"

"Audrey told me."

Audrey knew?

"She knew your mother didn't have heart trouble. She wanted an autopsy. So your father told her."

Which still doesn't explain—

"He didn't want to talk about it, she needed to talk about it, I was already aware of your mother's mental illness, so she told me."

It made sense. It was the first part of this whole thing that had made sense. It almost made too much sense.

Suddenly I realized why my mother would make a video, a question that had been moving under the surface of things since the second I saw her face but which didn't exactly surface until the answer bubbled up with it. She wanted somebody to talk to. She wanted to listen to her own voice speaking her worst fears so she could hear whether they sounded crazy, but she didn't know whom she could trust.

I said, "How am I supposed to know who to trust when I don't even trust myself?"

It was a hot day, but I was icy calm.

"Don't trust anybody," Laura said.

The Catholic girls filed into the building, and I got an image of it bursting into flames.

Once, the last Christmas Eve my mother was alive, my father gave us each a thousand dollars cash at nine o'clock in the morning and said, "Go to New Orleans, and don't come back until you've spent every penny, all on yourselves." And we fell for it. We jumped in the car, and late that night, we came back along the Mississippi instead of on I-10 because we wanted to stretch out our time together, away from my father, and in retrospect, I suspect he wanted the same thing. I suspect he and Audrey wanted some time with each other so they used me to make it happen for them. But people were lighting architectural bonfires along the river—it's a festival they have every year, and all through December people build elaborate wooden structures in the shapes of boats and castles and streetcars and, that year, a replica of the state Capitol building, and on Christmas Eve they pour gasoline on them and set them on fire.

I stopped the car, though we didn't get out, and we watched the Capitol light up in flames, in a beautiful rage. We watched it dance up into the night sky, screaming voiceless, sparkling howls like laughter and shouts of fear in dreams or cartoons, until it disappeared and crumpled in on itself, a pile of ashes, glowing. Then we drove back to Baton Rouge in absolute silence, barely even breathing.

When we walked in the Mansion, Audrey was there to greet us, full of eggnog and kisses, and my mother burst into a rage of angry, terrified tears, which I thought were because of the fire—I thought she'd seen it as a metaphor of herself, as I had, and I thought it had disturbed her as much as it did me—though later, of course, I came to suspect it was something else entirely. I had no idea why it didn't occur to me at the time, except that if it had, I would have thought, no, that's impossible. But all things are possible. If you can believe it, it's possible. That was a Bible verse on Jolie's wall.

Laura and I were both just sitting there, looking at the Capitol, as if we were waiting for something to burst into flames.

I picked up a leaf and started tearing it apart.

I said, "I just want the truth. I need to find a way to heal."

"Yes, you do," Laura said. "But it's putting too much faith in truth to believe that it can heal."

I didn't raise my voice. I didn't move. I kept looking forward, and I said, very calmly, "Maybe so, when truth is the difference between pancreatic cancer and some other disease. But it's not the same when the truth is the difference between suicide and murder."

Laura folded her arms on her chest, uncrossed her legs and recrossed them the other way, shifting her back to me. She was frustrated with me, but I didn't care. I was mad, too, and sick of people thinking they knew what I was going through when they had no idea, sick to death of it.

Or I did care—I cared about Laura—but she had the truth about her husband's death. She had X rays and ultrasound and biopsies and T-cell counts and test after test after test, all searching for the truth, and now that she had healed, years later, it wasn't her place to claim I didn't need the same certainty.

She looked up at the observation deck on top of the Capitol. The children were there by now, though we could barely see the tops of their heads, looking down on us and on Huey Long's grave there in the center of the front lawn.

I used to give tours. I'd start in the main lobby, where I told them about the marble from all around the world without mentioning that it was built at the height of the Depression, when people were starving. I told them how many jobs the construction provided Louisianans without saying how poorly they were paid. Then I'd lead them to the main hall, where I'd tell them about Huey Long's assassination. The boys always took turns hiding behind the column where Huey's assassin waited for him to step out of the elevator, jumping out and killing each other with imaginary guns, and the girls tended to focus on the black bullet scars in the granite floor and the granite walls, running their fingers over the wounds, counting them.

I didn't tell them the conspiracy theories. I didn't tell them how many rich people wanted Huey dead because of his plan to redistribute the wealth. I didn't tell them how many honest people wanted Huey dead because they were sick of Louisiana politics being for sale or how many vengeful people wanted him dead because he had systematically ruined the lives and careers of everybody who opposed him. I didn't tell them that Huey's hyped-up bodyguards may have shot him by accident when they thought they saw a man pull a gun. I told them the bodyguards killed the assassin, but I didn't mention that they shot sixty-two bullet holes through him, kept pumping lead into him for several minutes after he'd dropped his pistol and slumped to the floor in a pool of his own blood.

Then I'd lead them down the hall into the lobby of the legislative chambers and wait while they read the framed one-page-long list of crimes and misdemeanors Huey was charged with when he was threatened with impeachment, most of which he was probably guilty of but none of which he was convicted for. I told them that after the impeachment crisis passed—I didn't tell them how it passed, who was bought off with what threat, for what amount of money—just that after the crisis passed, Huey was elected to the U.S. Senate, and he was planning to run for President when he died. I left it to them to draw their own conclusions.

Then I took them to the observation deck on the roof, where they looked out over the monument to Huey Long on one side and the

Mississippi riverboat casinos on another, then the old armory building, last used during the Civil War, and the Governor's Mansion, and in the distance, church steeples and oil refineries and swamplands and suburbs, and they saw Louisiana as they'd never seen it before. Then I thanked them for coming and the tour was over, their education as cynics begun.

Laura stood up and started walking back toward the Capitol. She was upset—I could tell from behind, from the weight of her feet as they hit the concrete—and I didn't blame her. I was upset, too.

I hurried to catch up with her.

"I didn't mean that, about the cancer. I'm sorry, Laura. I shouldn't have said it. I was frustrated and I got off on the wrong subject, but I was just trying to get you to understand what I was saying, and I didn't think you did. So I got off on the wrong thing, but all I was trying to explain is why I think finding out the truth about the circumstances of my mother's death is a valid end unto itself, how it's something I need to do, whether I can justify it or not."

I was talking to her back, and I heard myself, sounding pitiful. I sounded like a pimply undergraduate philosophy major, and I didn't know myself whether I believed what I was saying or if I was just trying it on for size, but I said, "Don't you agree?" Something shrill in my voice made me sound like I was begging her.

She said, "Come with me."

I followed her up the stairs and into the lobby, then into the elevator and up to the observation deck. The last group of children got on the elevator as we got off, and we walked outside and around the corner and leaned into the guard wall. We looked out over the armory building toward the Mansion. Laura looked at the horizon, way in the distance, though there wasn't anything much to see. A few clouds, but I wasn't superstitious or poetic or whatever you have to be to find meaning in clouds on the horizon, and Laura was even less so.

She said, "The election's not far off now."

We were on top of the tallest building for miles, surrounded by nothing but sky, but I felt something pressing in on me.

I said, "Not too far."

She didn't move. She seemed to think she'd told me something I hadn't heard.

I said, "This has nothing to do with the campaign."

She said, with a hyper calmness, the way certain business people talk when they're very upset, "What kind of world do you think you live in, where the governor's daughter can run around the state capitol building telling people she thinks he murdered his wife, and it doesn't affect the campaign?"

"I am not running around telling people. I told you. But since you brought it up, if he did it, don't you think the people have a right to know who and what their candidate really is?"

"Ideally," Laura said, "every decision would be made based on full knowledge of all the facts on both sides."

"That's all I'm saying."

"But this is the real world," she said, "where all knowledge is partial knowledge and full disclosure on only one side of any issue is always a bad idea because what people don't know about the other side, they'll fill in with what they want to believe."

I hadn't given much thought to the other side in the campaign, mostly because I didn't think my father's only opponent, Michael King, posed much of a threat. Louisiana has open primaries, and the date to register as a candidate had passed quietly. Everybody with any real ambition was sitting the race out because my father's approval ratings were so high that they didn't have a chance, so I assumed King was just in it for the publicity. He was a former Klan leader who claimed to have found God, as all Klan members do, and changed his racist ways, as all racist politicians do, but when he talked about fixing education and fixing welfare and fixing health care without just throwing money at them, he meant screw all poor people of all races, a disproportionate number of which, in Louisiana, just happened to be black. So how else, besides running for office, is a guy like that going to get free air time?

Laura said, "If there were four or five other people running, I wouldn't give King a second look, but he's the only choice for everybody who's dissatisfied with the status quo, which is a hell of a lot of people."

I said, "Come on, Laura. I'm not saying there aren't any racists in Louisiana, but there aren't enough to elect King. Have you even looked at the polls?"

"Polls mean nothing if they aren't thermalized," adjusted to take liars and undecideds into account. "They're worse than meaningless because they let people get complacent. If they're polled, they'll say they're voting for your father because they know in their hearts that at worst, he's the lesser of two evils, but when they get in the booth and close the curtain, they've seen the same numbers and they think the election's all over, so anybody who's mad, anybody who feels alienated in any way, anybody who's heard rumors about your father's personal life that they don't approve of can think they're registering a protest vote that won't hurt anything, just send a message. Well, you get enough messages, you've got Michael King for governor, and we're all fucked."

I had an urge to throw myself off the building, a strong pull that felt like I was in danger of being thrown off by a force inside me that wasn't exactly me, the same irrational force that makes you afraid of turning the steering wheel hard to your right when you're driving over a bridge or taking the whole bottle of sleeping pills when you just need one. I backed away from the edge.

We walked around the corner, toward the door, and Laura stopped. We were facing the Mississippi. An empty barge was slowly passing. Two casino boats sat near the shore, the words *Casino Rouge* lit up like huge purple Christmas decorations, a celebration of the birth of Louisiana's new economic savior.

"Try to look at the big picture," Laura said.

That's what I'm trying to do.

"Your father could be the next President of the United States. It's a real possibility. He's got a lot of support from all over the country, and his name is starting to show up on a lot of people's short lists, so that's what's ultimately at stake here—not just your future or Carter's or even your father's, but the future history of our country and therefore the world. Think about it."

It was true.

So it wasn't exactly dishonest of her not to mention that her own ambitions were on the table as well. The plan was, my father would win the gubernatorial election and later step down to run for President, and Laura would become the governor, which was probably the best thing that could happen to Louisiana. I didn't know what was best for the rest of the world, and I didn't want to make the choice for them.

"Let's just say, hypothetically, that you're right, and he did it," she said. "I'm not saying I believe it—I don't—but let's just play what if."

"We don't have to."

A fighter plane roared over us so close I could feel it rumbling in my hair.

"Let's not even get to the presidential elections," she said. "Who would you rather be our next governor, a man who, hypothetically, killed one person but who's halfway through a renewal program that's providing jobs, education, and prenatal health care to more Louisianans than ever before, in effect saving hundreds, and long-term, thousands of lives, who has done more to lower violent crimes, improve race relations, and support women, gay, and minority entrepreneurs in this state than any previous governor in history? Or a man who isn't known to have killed anyone personally but who doesn't give a damn about the quality of life of the people he serves?"

"I get your point," I said.

Another fighter plane flew by—military practice runs.

Laura was still talking. "It's not just black people who'd suffer under him. How many corporations do you think would even consider locating their headquarters in a state with a leader of the Klan in the governor's office? How is a state with a governor like that going to begin to attract conventions, tourists, foreign investments? We'd be a laughingstock."

I hadn't been thinking in those terms. I was thinking about truth. Laura was talking consequences. So much for truth.

I turned around and walked inside. I headed toward the elevator and pressed the call button, and when Laura came and stood beside me, I pressed it again and again and again.

When we got in the elevator, I pressed L for lobby and we started going down. I couldn't see us moving, but I felt the motion in my gut and I paid attention to it so I wouldn't have to feel anything else there, and I watched the buttons light up. Twenty-two. Twenty-one. Twenty. We passed Laura's floor, but she didn't get off.

We passed Carter's and my father's floors, and she said, "So what are you going to do?"

"Nothing."

Laura just barely grunted and looked away. There was no pleasing her.

When we got outside, she walked down the stairs with me and followed me, walking beside me, to my car.

I leaned against the car, which felt hot on my skin through my skirt, and said, "Isn't that what you're asking me to do? Keep my hands clean and my mouth shut?"

She looked straight at me and said, "Doing nothing is not an option, because doing nothing is doing something. The state of the universe is such that we must act, but all action involves us in evil. So we fight it or work around it when we can, and we deal with it, even work with it, when we have to."

"But how do you know when you really have to or when saying you have to is just an excuse for doing what's convenient?"

"I don't think you always do. It's an imperfect world. Sometimes you just have to look at your choices, do what seems least wrong at the moment, and hope for the best."

Sometimes you tolerate murder. Sometimes you choose not to know what it is you're tolerating, because whatever it is, given your other options, you know you're still going to tolerate it.

"Okay, Laura," I said. I was unlocking my door. "You win. What do you want?"

She put her hand on mine, asking me not to go.

"I'm sorry," she said. "I'm sounding much more cynical than I am, but it's because I'm so certain that your father didn't do this and so intensely aware of the political ramifications of your suspicions— it's my job to be that way—but let's back up a minute. You came to me as a friend. And what was the first thing you said to me?"

"I don't know."

"You're confused, and understandably so."

"No, I'm not."

"No, that was the first thing you said to me, that you thought it might all be in your head. Listen to yourself. Trust that part of yourself."

"The part of me that says I'm crazy?"

"No, Grayson, you're not crazy. You're just under a tremendous amount of stress. You know your mother's problems weren't your fault, even though sometimes you feel guilty about them, and you're angry at your father for the same reasons almost everybody is angry at their father, so you want to blame him. That's a very normal reaction. But what you have to do now is look deep in your heart, set all your other hurts aside, and look to the truest place in yourself and ask, do I really believe this man who has committed his life to public service—"

This politician, in other words.

"This basically good, decent person who loved your mother, stood by her for thirty-seven years—and yes, sometimes he wasn't easy to live with, but neither was she—and he stayed with her, got her the best medical care in the world, and did his damnedest to make a terminally unhappy woman happy. Now, do you seriously believe that after all that, he would turn around and kill her? Murder her in cold blood? Does that even sound believable?"

I hadn't smoked in three years, not since my divorce, but I suddenly wanted a cigarette. I wanted to light it while it was in my mouth, feel the flame from the lighter hot on my face, and I wanted to take in all the smoke my lungs could stand and hold it there until I could feel it cool and calm and cancerous in my brain.

I said, "No."

"Are you sure? Don't just say it for my benefit. I want you to be totally honest with yourself."

"Yeah."

Then I'd let out the smoke, long and slow, and watch it disappear.

"Do you love your father?"

"Of course."

"I know you do. And he loves you. So do this much. It's not any more than what the criminal courts do for their defendants: assume he's innocent. Assume his innocence until and unless you are presented with clear and incontrovertible proof of his guilt, beyond any reasonable doubt."

I'd tap the ashes against the edge of the bench and let them fall to the ground.

I said, "Okay." I meant it.

Laura said, "It's your moral obligation, and his moral and legal right."

"Okay."

The cigarette would be resting between my fingers, smoldering at the tip, consuming itself.

"And don't just act on that assumption. Believe in it. Live with it, breathe it, wake and sleep with it, take comfort from it."

I'd take another drag.

I felt hot and sweaty and sort of numb and hypersensitive at the same time, like when you're hungover, which I wasn't, but it felt like something that started out as pleasure had turned toxic inside me.

She said, "And redirect all this creative energy that you've been using to make up murder plots into helping your father get re-elected."

Her voice sounded slightly irritated, but she caressed my hair gently, moved her hand from my head to my neck and down my spine until it came to rest between my shoulder blades, and I tried not to stiffen.

I tried to tell myself it was a gesture of affection, but who's to say what's true? Maybe it was also a warning. Maybe there was a reason she was pressing her hand right where somebody would stab me in the back if they were aiming for my heart.

WHEN I GOT HOME, I HID THE GUN INSIDE one of a pair of black velvet boots I'd bought on sale and never worn.

Carter and I ate dinner at the Mansion that night, a spur-of-the-moment invitation from my father. We had boiled crawfish in the downstairs family dining room, and a bowl full of heads and empty bodies sat in front of each of our plates. Audrey and I were just eating the tails, but Carter and my father were sucking the brains out of theirs. It's a Cajun delicacy, every bit as disgusting as it sounds.

Audrey sat across from me, in my mother's chair, where she'd sat at every meal we'd eaten there since my mother died, which suddenly bothered me. She looked more like my mother every time I saw her, a younger, prettier version of my mother, with better skin and better hair and more makeup, and that bothered me, too. I was afraid I was forgetting what my mother looked like, replacing her in my mind's eye with Audrey.

She also looked like me, an older version of me.

As soon as I start seeing Audrey when I look in the mirror, I'm going to have plastic surgery—face-lift, eye job, cheek implants, liposuction, the works. I should start saving my money now.

That's where my mind was. I'd made my decision about what I was going to do—assume they're all innocent—and I was trying to put my cloak-and-dagger days behind me.

Carter and my father and Audrey were talking about the press conference, the one Carter and I had watched two days earlier while me made love, before I played the video—a lifetime ago. My father's numbers had been way up since my mother died—sympathy ratings—and they'd jumped two points since the press conference. The people had accepted Audrey as my father's wife, even though the marriage had occurred just two months after my mother's funeral, which amounted to a rejection of my mother, or at least an easy acceptance of her death.

My father took Audrey's hand and said, "We could go all the way now," meaning the White House.

Carter lifted his glass in a toast to the White House, and Audrey and my father lifted theirs with him, all smiles, and what hung in the air unsaid and unrefuted, irrefutable, was that it could happen with Audrey, where it hadn't been possible with my mother.

When the idea of their getting married first came up, Carter argued that they should have waited until after the election—I thought they shouldn't have done it at all—but nobody could tell my father anything, so once a date had been set, Carter, the ultimate pragmatist, was all for it. Choose your battles, he'd say, and know when you've lost. Translation: When you can't win, figure out that you're going to lose before your opponent does so you can switch sides before the battle's over and take credit for the victory.

I took a sip of beer, a bite of bread.

My father was still touching Audrey's hand. I wanted him to stop, which I realized was unfair and irrational, but I figured I had a right to an irrational emotion or two as long as I didn't express it, which I didn't. I just sat there and ate.

Carter sucked a head.

There was a lag in the conversation, but I didn't care.

Then my father said, "Audrey?"

He was prompting her, and she forced a smile, and Carter straightened in his chair.

I'm the only one here who doesn't know what's coming next.

Audrey dipped her fingers in a bowl of lemon water, wiped them off with a napkin, and said, "So anyway, Grayson, I was hoping you'd be willing to continue on as assistant to the First Lady, although, of course, your job would be very"—then she searched around for a word before she landed on "different." Then she added, "now."

I looked at my father.

He said, "We want to keep you on salary and not have to face any messy questions about what your job responsibilities have been for the last few months"—a low blow, since I was still drawing a paycheck for taking care of my mother—"and of course, Audrey feels like you know the ropes, you could show her around."

Audrey said to my father, "I sure do."

Carter said to me, "Well, you *do*."

The room was very quiet. Everybody had stopped eating.

I didn't have a choice—you don't say no to my father—and we all knew it. Though I would have said yes at that point even if it had been up to me and the question of my paycheck hadn't been raised. Do my part.

I said, "Sure."

My father said, "So you're on the team?"

It was an odd question. As far as my father knew, I'd never been off the team.

I said, "Of course."

Go team.

Laura wasn't there and her name hadn't come up, but I wondered if the three of them knew I'd gone to see her and if so, how much else they knew.

Maybe I shouldn't have trusted her. She told me herself not to trust anybody. Though she also told me to trust my father's innocence.

"Excellent," my father said.

Audrey said, "Wonderful."

Carter said, "Great."

They all started eating again, my father and Carter barely chewing their food before they swallowed it, like predators.

At least they're not trying to kill me. They wouldn't have offered me a job if they were trying to kill me.

I knew it was a strange thing to think.

These are the people who love me most in the world.

I felt like crying.

These are the people I love.

I took another bite of bread.

"Pass the salad," I said.

I was back on my diet.

Carter said something not terribly funny, and Audrey laughed long and loud, and her laugh reminded me of an ambulance.

My father touched my fingers when he handed me the salad, he pressed them, and I looked at his face to see if he did it on purpose—he almost never touched me—and he met my eyes and smiled slyly at me, as if we'd just made a deal.

I've seen that smile before.

It was more than a year earlier, a year before my mother died, the Saturday before Mardi Gras day, when New Orleans is so full of people dressed in outrageous costumes or barely dressed at all and everybody's mind is so far off politics that public figures can walk around virtually unnoticed, and my father and I met for lunch at the Bistro at Maison de Ville. We had an unspoken agreement not to tell my mother we'd been in New Orleans and we didn't discuss the reasons we hadn't invited her or the reasons we weren't telling her. At that point, I wasn't telling anybody the whole truth about where and with whom I spent my time—I was seeing a married man—and I thought my father just needed some time away from her and wanted some time alone with me. I thought it was that simple for him, maybe because I wanted it to be that simple. I was starting to feel overly complicated and fragmented, like my whole life was nothing but a series of lies.

My father said, "How do you think your mother's doing?"

"About the same, maybe a little worse," I said, suddenly upset at the truth of it. I was much more comfortable lying, especially about her. I drank some water and took a bite of bread to keep from bursting into tears.

He put his hand on top of mine, something he'd done maybe four times in my life. His hands were big and warm and I wanted him not to stop touching me, never to stop, though at the same time I felt vaguely uncomfortable about how we must have looked—a handsome, sixty-year-old man in an Armani suit and a thirty-three-year-old woman holding hands over lunch in a secluded restaurant.

His bodyguards were sitting at the table next to ours, watching every move we made.

He said, "She can be exhausting. I don't know how I'd survive without your help," and I felt something open up in me like a wound. It was the first time in my life I'd ever understood that my father needed me, need being almost as good as love in some ways. I felt something red like rage or exhilaration or an emotion I couldn't name coursing through me like wine or rushing out of me like blood. It scared me. I was starting to feel empty, emptied, so I tried to stop the flow, press something closed inside myself.

Okay, I probably could have avoided a lot of mistakes in my life if I'd known this earlier, but that's past, and what matters is that I know it now.

I took a deep breath and took back my hand and said, "Thanks."

I said the alphabet in my head. I said the books of the Bible. Then I counted the ice cubes in my glass. Seven. They were small ice cubes. I was trying not to think about my mother. I took another bite of bread, and I thought of Jesus breaking bread and saying, "Do this in remembrance of me," which suddenly didn't make sense at all.

What part of this is supposed to remind a person of God?

I felt like I was missing something important.

When our food came, we ate ravenously without speaking, as if we'd said all there was in the world to say.

After lunch, my father told me he had to get back to Baton Rouge for business. I didn't question what business there was to do on the Saturday before Mardi Gras. I didn't even wonder.

I told him I'd called a girlfriend to roam around the Quarter with me for a few hours.

And fifteen minutes later, I met my lover on the steps of the Cathedral, and soon we were walking side by side down Orleans toward the Bourbon Orleans Hotel. I wanted to take his hand, but we were waiting to touch until we were alone, enjoying the wait. We stopped to watch a street musician, a tenor saxophone shaping sounds like rushing water and muffled screams and the way it feels to want to make love when you know your lover doesn't love you. I felt a flush of irritation at a man dressed in a spandex skeleton who walked past us and turned the corner onto Bourbon Street—he didn't have any bones in the back, just black spandex. Then I saw a man who looked like my father go into the Bourbon Orleans and I felt another flush of irritation at that, though I dismissed the thought as impossible—my father was in Baton Rouge, not to mention the man in the hotel wasn't being followed by body-guards.

When the saxophonist finished, he took off his hat, asking for money. We gave him a couple dollars, but most people started shuffling away as if they'd never even stopped to listen. Some jerk down the street was eating fire, which doesn't take any talent, just a kind of recklessness, and raking in the bucks. The saxophonist pressed his hat toward the tourists, yelling, "I have to eat. Don't you know I have to eat like everybody else?"

We went inside, where jazz floated in from the courtyard, another saxophonist moving into something like musical tears, which, as with all crying in public, made me uncomfortable, and the man I was about to sleep with went to get our key. So I was waiting in the lobby, sitting in a maroon velvet chair that looked like it belonged in a bordello, eating a goldfish cracker and feeling vaguely uneasy, wanting to be alone and wanting to be held, when I saw my father.

My impeccably dressed father—and I'd thought he'd dressed up for me—he walked to the elevator and pushed the button and took a room key out of his jacket pocket. We'd picked the same hotel for the same reasons—it's elegant but big and busy and you can feel anonymous there, while most rooms in the heart of the Quarter are in little inns and B&Bs where they learn your name when you arrive—and my face went hot with fear: *As different as I am from him in some ways, I'm just like him in others.*

I was fighting the feeling that my whole life, every choice I'd ever make, was already written out for me by my father and I was following a script I'd never read. I had a mental image like a split screen on the news of my father undressing some woman in one room and my lover undressing me in another, identical room on an identical bed. The woman with my father was about my age and she was pret-

ELIZABETH DEWBERRY

tier than my mother, prettier than me but with similar features, and I felt something like hatred for her, though I had no idea and didn't want to know who she was.

The man I was about to make love to was walking across the lobby toward me—he hadn't seen my father—and I didn't know what he'd told his wife about where he was, but I suddenly realized if anybody ever asked where my father had been that day, I was his alibi.

The courtyard saxophonist circled into a rushing-water vamp like the one we'd heard earlier on the street, except he pitched his in a lower key, like an undercurrent, and he was playing it faster so he sounded desperate. I was feeling desperate and the elevator was running slow and my father was tapping his key card against his thigh, anxious to go up. Then he turned around for no reason, almost like he was stretching his neck, and our eyes met and he smiled that same sly smile—we'd both been caught in lies, and the explanations were all too obvious—and I found myself smiling back at him because I couldn't think of anything else to do. And instantly, without a word passing between us, we'd made a tacit agreement about how we were going to deal with it: *We will keep each other's secrets.*

When the elevator doors opened, he turned away from me and stepped in. We never mentioned it again.

I didn't even speak of it to the man I was with. We just went to our room and made love until we were sweating and exhausted and empty, and after, in the shower, I started crying and told him I couldn't do this anymore, it was wrong and it was tearing me apart.

He said he understood, he would always think sweet thoughts of me. I couldn't tell if he was being incredibly considerate or if it just hadn't meant that much to him in the first place. Then we dressed and kissed goodbye and left separately. We didn't see each other again except at public functions and fund-raisers, where he always brought his wife.

And that night at the Mansion, well over a year later, my father was smiling his same sly smile across the dinner table, and I found myself smiling back just as I had before, though I told myself I had no idea what kind of deal we'd just made.

So I KEPT MY PROMISES, DID MY PART. ALL summer, I campaigned for my father, tried not to think too much or too hard about my mother. Carter hired a private investigator to dig up dirt on King just in case we needed it, and every time I felt tempted to look for evidence of anybody's guilt—my father's, Dr. Fontenot's, Carter's, or even my own—I told myself King must have hired his own people, ruthless people, to investigate us. If there was anything left to find out about my mother's death, they'd find it.

It was always a temptation, though. For reasons I didn't understand but that made me feel ashamed, I *wanted* to look for evidence. Part of me even wanted to find it. Which seemed to confirm my suspicion that I was willfully, if sort of subconsciously, looking for excuses to ruin what was good in all our lives—Carter's and mine, but also my father's and even Audrey's. I'd thought about calling off the wedding, which would have raised a zillion questions I couldn't have begun to answer, even to myself, and which wouldn't have solved anything.

Evidence of the same pattern, I told myself.

So I determined to control my self-destructive impulses the same way my mother should have controlled hers. I didn't see a therapist, but I read several self-help books and tried to do what they said. The premise of one of them was that everything we do is motivated by either love or fear, which oversimplified things, but which also seemed true: I knew my mother was driven by fear, destroyed by it, and I didn't want to live that way. If you can choose to live in love, I wanted to. One said, "All you're responsible for is what isn't right in you. You can't fix what's wrong with everybody else, and you shouldn't try." Which also held some truth, not to mention comfort.

Let the bad parts go. Focus on what's good.

So the last Saturday in August, I married Carter.

It was a simple ceremony at the Mansion. No press. We wrote our own vows. I carried wildflowers.

We'd decided to buy a new house, but we put the house and even the honeymoon off until after the election. And all of September and October, we spent twelve-hour days, seven days a week, traveling to every parish in Louisiana, living and breathing, eating and sleeping nothing but getting my father re-elected. It was exhilarating, having such a clear sense of purpose and passion, not having time to second-guess anything, in some ways more like a honeymoon than a honeymoon would have been.

Most of what was reported in the press was inaccurate, either from journalists' apathy or their incompetence, but not inaccurate enough to matter. We didn't make an issue of the lies in King's autobiography or his affiliation with the Klan, partly because we knew the national media were watching and we didn't want it to look like the voters had had no real choice, but mostly because the newspapers kept bringing it up for us.

Voter turnout was low, but my father won by a landslide. The victory and especially the margin turned some heads at national party headquarters and got us stories in *Time* and *Newsweek* and *The New York Times*, all of which mentioned my father as a presidential contender. *Time* said he'd need to raise twenty-five million dollars first, but my father had already hired a consultant who'd said, "Don't announce your candidacy until the American people feel like it was their idea and you're just accepting their call. One step at a time."

So as soon as the election was over, we started planning for a week of inauguration parties and pageantry and photo-ops that, we hoped, would help spark the idea in the American people's minds that my father should be their next President. And as soon as the first guests arrived at the first party, my father, Audrey, and Carter started working the room the way fish work a tank when they're feeding.

It was the plan, but I'd had enough, and I was tired. I was tired of shaking rich people's hands, laughing at rich people's jokes. I felt intensely lonely, surrounded by strangers. I wanted to be in my own house, alone, with somebody who knew me and loved me—which was exactly what my mother would have felt and what I would have resented her for feeling. I was beginning to realize how little I'd understood her. I felt like I was *becoming* her in certain ways.

So I spent most of the cocktail hour watching Dr. Fontenot hold court with several older women whose husbands were ignoring them, while his wife stayed outside on the back patio, smoking cigarettes and drinking vodka martinis, not talking to anybody.

He told a joke about a duck and a man with a hard-on who walked into a bar, and the three women who were hanging on him at that point smiled and twittered as if they were embarrassed but happy to be so, and I laughed out loud. Then he was suddenly quiet, and he looked straight at me and said, "You remind me more of Marie every day."

I felt myself blushing, which I hadn't done in years, and I said, "Thank you."

I wanted to say more to him, though I wasn't sure what, and for him to say more to me, but there were too many people standing around. So I just smiled.

When he started into another joke, I was playing what he'd said over in my mind.

You remind me of your mother.

Coming from Carter, it would have felt like a warning, but from Dr. Fontenot, it made me feel good about who I was and who my mother had been.

Maybe it was that simple—she liked what she saw when she looked at herself through his eyes.

I was trying not to think it had anything to do with the Kama Sutra.

Dr. Fontenot went outside, out the front door, though his wife was still in the back. Carter took my arm and introduced me to several of Louisiana's most generous millionaires—he'd started throwing around the idea of running for Congress.

As soon as I could, I followed Dr. Fontenot out.

He was standing at the end of the veranda by himself, leaning against a column, looking toward the Capitol and smoking a cigarette. He held his pack of cigarettes out to me, but I smiled back and shook my head. It was the first time I'd been alone with him all evening. It may have been the first time ever.

I said, "Tell me about my mother."

He didn't answer me right away.

"I know you loved her."

He turned toward me.

"I'm glad you did," I said. "I'm sure that kept her alive."

His eyebrows were tensed together, and there was something like surprise or alarm or maybe concern on his face.

I said, "Well, I mean, for as long as she *was* alive, it kept her alive. I didn't mean anything more complicated than that. I wanted to know how I'm like her."

He dropped his cigarette butt on the ground, crushed it under his shoe.

"I'm sorry," I said. "I've made you uncomfortable."

He said, "I wish she were here, too." He said it softly, then lit another cigarette.

I wanted to touch him, to squeeze his hand or put my head on his shoulder, but I didn't. I just stood there. We stood there together.

It was January, but it was a warm night.

Dr. Fontenot took a long drag and let it out slowly, and I breathed in his smoke. We stood for a long time on the veranda looking at the Capitol lit up against the night sky, connected by smoke and by silence, by all the things we couldn't say. The band inside played "You Are My Sunshine," then something sad I didn't recognize.

We didn't say a word until a mosquito landed on my arm, and I said, "Oh," and slapped it. It left a bright spot of blood on my skin, and Dr. Fontenot dropped his cigarette on the ground and said, "Here," and dabbed off the blood with his cocktail napkin. Our voices sounded loud and awkward, as if they'd broken some kind of spell.

I said, "Thank you," the same thing I'd said when he told me I reminded him of my mother. I felt disappointed and stupid and more empty than ever.

"Mosquitoes in January," he said.

I said, "That's Louisiana for you."

I didn't mean anything by it, but it came out sounding cynical. My arm was itching, and I was hot. I wanted to go inside.

Dr. Fontenot said, "How did you find out?"

I didn't want to tell him about the things in the attic. I didn't want to tell him anything, especially since he hadn't told me anything about my mother, even after I'd practically begged, though another part of me wanted to tell him everything and ask him to explain it to me, make him explain it all away.

I said, "From my mother."

Dr. Fontenot said, "I didn't know you knew, and I didn't think it was my place to tell you."

He still wasn't going to tell me anything.

I was feeling stuck inside my skin, and I wanted to move out of myself, into Carter's arms. I wanted Carter to touch me and open me up and fill me with light until I felt like I was floating. It had been a long time since I'd felt that way.

Dr. Fontenot said, "Not a day goes by that I don't think of her. I would give anything . . ." Then he exhaled, and the rest of that sentence was a shake of his head. When he lit a new cigarette, his fingers were just barely trembling.

I touched his elbow to offer some comfort, but my touch startled him. I pulled back and said, "I'm sorry."

He said, "God forgive us all." His voice was trembling.

Then he crossed himself quickly, privately, as he'd done the night my mother died.

Inside, the band stopped playing, and a light went out somewhere, and I felt something dark melting inside me, melting over me, and I looked at his face.

God forgive us for what?

He wouldn't look at me.

Tell me we're innocent. Tell me I'm right to assume your innocence.

He turned away from me and stared out toward the Capitol, though I had a feeling he wasn't seeing anything except whatever was in his own mind. The smoke from his cigarette smelled bitter and comforting, and the breeze off the lake was warm and cool, and I felt very big and very small. He closed his eyes. He could have been thinking of my mother or maybe praying, but then he flinched and closed his eyes tighter, as if he were in pain.

I said, "Dr. Fontenot?" I didn't know what I was going to say next.

He turned toward me. It was dark, but his face didn't look like its normal color, and he was sweating—I was afraid he was having a heart attack—and I said, "Are you okay?"

Carter stepped outside before Dr. Fontenot could answer me. I heard somebody through the open door talking into a microphone, and Carter walked over to us and said, "Where have you been?"

"Right here," I said.

Dr. Fontenot pulled himself out of wherever he'd been. He patted his forehead dry with the same cocktail napkin he'd used to wipe off my blood and muttered something about having needed some air.

I said, "Yeah, just catching a breath."

I took Carter's hand, and we went inside.

Dr. Fontenot avoided me the rest of the evening.

In the car on our way home Carter said, "What did you talk about with Mike Fontenot?"

I didn't want to tell him what Dr. Fontenot had said on the veranda, so I said, "Nothing. Stupid stuff. Mosquitoes."

"You talked all that time without saying a thing?"

"Well, that's how saying nothing works. If you say nothing quickly, then you've actually said something. Depending on the context, you can say 'welcome' or 'fuck off' without opening your mouth, but if you stand around saying next to nothing for most of a cocktail party, that's when you're really saying nothing."

Carter didn't answer me.

Then he said, "Okay, fine."

The temperature had dropped, and I turned on the heater as high as it would go.

After a few minutes, Carter turned it off.

I turned it back on, though, and he left it that way. I couldn't get comfortable.

I was trying to figure Carter out, trying to come up with an explanation for his questions, and trying to convince myself that what Dr. Fontenot had wanted God's forgiveness for was having an affair with my mother, not anything worse than that. Which didn't work, because having an affair didn't involve me, although maybe the other person in us was my mother, but who was the *all* in *God forgive us all* unless *it was all our sins.*

Maybe what he meant was, God have mercy on us all, because we all miss her, except that nobody asks for forgiveness unless they're guilty, so what if he helped my father kill her? And if he was, then Carter was asking what we were talking about because he thought I might find out what Dr. Fontenot knew, which terrified him.

Which terrified me.

Because the same logic that made Carter and my father innocent if Dr. Fontenot was innocent, made them guilty if he was guilty. Neither could or would have done it without the others' help.

You killed her. You all killed her. We killed her. God damn us all.

I let the idea sit low in my stomach for a while. I was waiting to see if it would go away on its own, like when you think you have food poisoning but it turns out to be stress, which was a version of what had happened every time the idea had come up since I'd promised Laura to leave the subject alone.

The part of me that was well read in the ways of mourning and well practiced in the ways of rationalizing was trying to convince the rest of me that Dr. Fontenot's comment about God's forgiveness was just the kind of detail I'd blown out of proportion for no reason after I first watched the video, an old, grief-related obsession that was resurfacing simply because I was grieving again in anticipation of both my mother's absence at the inauguration and the upcoming absence of purpose in my own life as soon as the inauguration was over.

Though another part of me couldn't stop seeing something dark there, dark enough to disappear into, and I felt that darkness descending over me, wrapping itself around me, so tight I was having trouble filling my lungs. I turned off the heater and rolled down the window so I could breathe the night in. I looked at the sky, at the dark between the stars.

I was arguing with myself.

Carter didn't kill her.

Of course not.

No, you didn't literally kill her, but you know who did, and you knew the night they did it, and you covered for them then and you've been covering for them ever since and there's no going back because there's no fucking way to explain why you didn't say anything until now.

I thought I was talking to Carter in my head, silently screaming at him, but then I realized I was also accusing myself.

I killed her. I let her die when I could have saved her, and I let the people who committed the actual murder get away with it. I destroyed the key evidence, and then I closed my eyes and kept my mouth shut, and now she's dead and we all have to live with that, and we all deserve to die.

God have mercy on us all.

I was wearing my seat belt, and I put my hand on the cross strap where it was pressing on my chest—I could feel my heart pounding through it—and I held onto the strap, trying to keep myself from jumping out of the car. I was also fighting the urge to grab the steering wheel and slam us head-on into a tree, totaling the car and killing us both, and the most convincing argument I could make to myself about why I shouldn't do it was that Carter had air bags, so it wouldn't work.

I wasn't drunk, but I wasn't sober. I wasn't moving, but I couldn't make myself be still.

If there was a way to make yourself disappear, I would figure it out right now.

When we got home, Carter took off his clothes and lay down on the bed in his underwear and socks and turned on the TV.

I went in the bathroom.

I turned on the shower for privacy and got out the notepad and pen Carter kept in a drawer by the toilet, where he got his best ideas, and wrote, "Dear Carter." My hand was shaking—the letters looked misshapen—and I didn't know what was coming next, if it was going to be a Dear John letter where I said I was leaving him or a suicide note, but I was absolutely certain that I wasn't going to wake up in Carter's bed the next morning.

I felt scared and confused and very focused, the way it feels to drive through dense fog at night, where it takes all your effort to see a tiny moment into your own future, and there are no decisions to make, just mistakes to avoid, fatal mistakes.

I COULDN'T THINK OF ANYTHING ELSE TO write, though, so I took off my clothes and got in the shower. Suicide notes don't make sense. If you still have something left to say and somebody worth saying it to, why kill yourself?

I started counting pills in my head.

4 Ambien
20 Xanax, more or less
1½ bottles of over-the-counter sleeping pills

I didn't know if that would kill a person or not.

It would be better if I had some vodka, but I'd have to go through the bedroom to the kitchen to get it, and I don't want to talk to Carter. I'm not going to explain if he asks me what I'm doing, and I don't want to tell him any more lies, and I don't want him to go into the bathroom while I'm in the kitchen getting the vodka because I can't take the pills into the kitchen without looking suspicious, but he can spend twenty minutes in here at a time doing God knows what, and if I'm going to do this, I want to do it now.

I thought about praying, giving myself some sort of last rites, but it didn't make sense, asking God for help at that point. If you still believe God might help you out, why kill yourself, but if you don't believe it, why pray?

I scrubbed myself hard. I wanted to be as clean as possible if I killed myself, so the mortician wouldn't have to give me a bath. I was hoping I had enough food in my stomach but not so much that I'd throw up and calculating how much water I'd have to drink to swallow all the pills and worrying that the water would dilute everything else and trying to imagine what it would feel like to die. I didn't think it would hurt, but I wasn't afraid if it did. I've always had a high tolerance for pain.

The only thing that surprised me was how beautifully simple and straightforward it all seemed. I couldn't imagine why I hadn't thought of it that way before.

What was complicated was that it wasn't the only thing going on in my brain. I had several monologues going in my head at once, like an opera with many arias, except that nothing harmonized. An orchestra before the symphony. The loudest voice was counting pills, but the next loudest was saying, *Now that I'm in my mother's shoes, about to kill myself, whatever reasons I've told myself she couldn't have done it because I didn't see it coming don't make quite as much sense, because I didn't exactly see this coming either. But now that I'm here, it feels like I've been moving in this direction all my life. So I can see how she might have felt the same things I'm feeling, done what I'm about to do. Although if she did, then neither Carter nor my father nor Dr. Fontenot nor I did it to her, so if I'm killing myself because we did, then I'm doing it for nothing.*

Another, slightly softer voice was thinking how pissed Carter would be that I'd spent so much money redecorating the house and then killed myself anyway, while an even fainter voice was trying to remind me that there were times I'd felt like killing myself before—though I couldn't think exactly when at that moment—and after they'd passed, I'd told myself, *Remember this, remember being glad you're not dead.*

The closest, quietest voice, was saying, *Okay, Grayson, you're going to let yourself have this little temper tantrum, but you're not stupid or selfish or crazy enough to take it further than that. Especially not less than a week before the inauguration. So you're going to get up tomorrow where you're supposed to, in Carter's bed, and do what you've done all your life, exactly what everybody expects you to do. You'll pretend nothing's wrong. You'll smile for the cameras, nod to the reporters, greet the guests, and help your father move a big step closer to the White House. And chances are, things will turn out all right. Everything will be fine.*

Things were quieting down.

It was after midnight.

I got out of the shower, took one Xanax to help me sleep, and stuffed my abortive suicide note to the bottom of the wastebasket. Then I put on my nightgown and got in bed.

Carter was already asleep.

I turned out the lights.

I felt the way it feels to rise up out of water, the cling and the pull of the emptiness left behind.

THE NEXT MORNING, I SLEPT LATE, AND BY the time I woke up, Carter was already out of bed and showered.

I pulled on a robe and went in the living room, where he was feeding frozen bloodworms to the fish.

I said, "Hi."

He looked up. "How are you feeling?"

"A little ragged around the edges."

He said, "Are you okay?"

He seemed genuinely concerned, which made me suspicious.

"I'm fine," I said. "I'm just sleepy."

Carter wasn't acting hungover, and I didn't want him to know I was if he wasn't.

My eyelids felt heavy and puffy, as if I'd cried the night before, though I didn't think I had. I couldn't remember every single minute.

I yawned and forced a smile and said, "How long have you been up?"

"An hour, hour and a half. Want some coffee?"

"Yeah."

He said, "I'll get it."

I followed him into the kitchen and watched him grab the portable phone off the kitchen table without missing a step and put it in its cradle on his way to the coffeemaker. He'd obviously been talking on the phone, which wouldn't have raised a question in my mind—Carter always talked on the phone—except that he apparently didn't want me to know he had.

He was pouring my coffee.

I said, "What have you been doing?"

"Nothing. Reading the paper."

He handed me the coffee.

I said, "Thanks."

I was standing in the kitchen doorway, leaning against the door frame.

"Come here," he said. He took my hand, and we went in the living room and sat down in front of the fish. We were quiet for a while. I wanted some aspirin. I put my head on his shoulder.

I said, "The fish look good."

We'd been so busy, we'd been ignoring them. You never know when saltwater fish are going to drop dead. In a predator tank, fish who've been living peacefully together for years but who aren't getting enough of whatever they want—food or space or even attention—can start fighting one day and kill each other.

He said, "I've been thinking."

Then he stopped, which meant something bad was coming. I didn't know if he was genuinely reluctant to be the bearer of bad news or if he was being manipulative, making me ask for it, but I knew it was bad.

I said, "About what?"

He hesitated. Then he said, "There's this bluebird wrasse at the fish store that's absolutely beautiful. I think we should go down there and get it."

Which wasn't where I thought he'd been going.

I said, "Today?"

He said, "I know, Pablo would probably try to kill him"—his Picasso, a territorial triggerfish that had killed the last two fish he'd tried to put in the tank.

"He probably would," I said.

"But I'm thinking maybe the wrasse is big enough that he could hold his own."

"I don't know," I said. "It's just so upsetting when they die." The last one suffered for days. Eventually, Carter had to euthanize it, which had bothered both of us.

We didn't say anything for a while.

Then he said, "Maybe you should get some medication." Which sounded like a change in direction but which was where we'd been heading all along.

I took a sip of coffee.

I said, "For what?"

"Depression."

He said it as casually as anybody could possibly say "depression." Too casually.

My coffee was cold. I put the mug on the coffee table.

I said, "But I'm not depressed."

He said, "Well, you're not over your mother's death. It's been almost a year."

We were sitting there, very still. The only thing moving in the room was our voices. Our voices, and the fish, but they were behind a glass wall, where their movements didn't make any sound and barely seemed like a part of this world. I felt like a part of me was trapped behind a wall, too, where nobody could hear it or touch it or keep it from dying.

I said, "You've said yourself I'm in denial about Mother. Well, the one thing denial has going for it is that you can't be depressed if you're in it."

"Calm down, Grayson. I'm just trying to help."

"I am calm. You calm down. You're the one who's blowing things out of proportion."

We were still sitting on the sofa, but it felt like we'd moved to a different place, a place I'd never been. I wanted to get up and walk out, but I made myself stay there.

He said, "Are you still having nightmares?"

"No. Come to think of it, I'm not dreaming at all."

"Well, last night, you sat up in bed and said, 'God forgive us all.' "

"I did?"

"Yes."

Carter kept talking, but I stopped listening. Part of me didn't believe him, but how could he have made it up? And why? The only other way he could know is if Dr. Fontenot told him our whole conversation.

Carter said, "Not dreaming, feeling excessive guilt, difficulty concentrating, impaired analytical thinking, inability to stop mourning, drinking too much—these are all classic symptoms of depression, which is a very treatable illness."

"I'm thinking quite clearly," I said, "and I'm not having any trouble concentrating. Where did you come up with this?"

"Sometimes I look over at you when you're supposed to be working, and you seem a million miles away."

I laughed, sort of, and said, "You're not happy with my work? This is about work?"

He said, "That's not what I'm saying. You're doing a great job, but you don't seem happy. I want to make you happy."

I felt like screaming, *I am happy, dammit, so why don't you just shut up and stop trying to make me anything.*

Which, I realized, would have sounded like the ravings of a lunatic, so I didn't scream anything.

I felt the way it feels in dreams underwater when you're swimming around panicking, trying to find air, but you can't, although everybody around you is breathing normally, so you're also trying to act like nothing's wrong.

I drank some more coffee, though I was wide awake.

I was trying to be logical and objective and honest with myself.

I said, "Well, for starters, happy and not depressed are two different things. But even, hypothetically, if I were depressed, it takes six weeks to get an appointment with a psychologist and another three to six weeks for Prozac to work, and whatever I'm going through, I'm sure I'll be over it by then."

He said, "Zoloft works faster than that."

The room was very quiet. The fish tank was making white noise, humming without making music. Carter was holding my hand.

I said, "How fast?"

"A few days, usually, sometimes overnight. And you don't have to wait for an appointment. I can get it for you."

"When?"

"Now."

"Today?"

"It might take a couple of days, but not six weeks."

Everything stopped—the argument in my head, the silent laughing and crying and screaming.

I said, "I don't want to go on Zoloft, Carter. I'm not crazy. I'm not chemically imbalanced. I'm just in mourning, which is very normal—what's not normal is not mourning at all—and I want to get through this on my own."

"I know you're not crazy," he said. "But if you need some help, that's normal, too. Anytime, you just say the word."

I didn't say anything. I had some more questions, but I didn't want to ask them. I was afraid of the answers.

He said, "Just keep it in mind."

"Okay."

I went in the kitchen and started washing dishes. Not exactly washing—just putting them in the sink under running water, scraping off the hardened cheese and dried guacamole and wilted lettuce from three or four nights before. Carter followed me. He was helping, or he thought he was. He was moving things from one counter to another, closer to the sink.

I said, "Whose idea was this?"

The sink was full, and I turned off the water.

He said, "What do you mean? Suggesting that somebody who's depressed go on antidepressants is hardly a brainstorm. Why don't you just try it for a few weeks, see how you feel? Why not give yourself a break?"

I was about to say, *Because, as I told you forty seconds ago, I'm not depressed.*

Then I thought, *Okay, fine, believe I'm depressed since apparently that's what you want to believe. And tell my father, who will tell Audrey, and later, when I feel better, if you all decide I'm manic, then believe that, too.*

I said, "Who would supply the drugs?"

"You're making this sound like I'm running a cocaine ring. It's one of the safest medications on the market."

The counters were clean, but he sprayed them with disinfectant.

Leaves were falling outside.

I said, "I just want to know where you'd get the Zoloft if I said yes. That's a fair question."

He said, "Mike Fontenot."

He said it with the same deliberate casual tone he'd first used when he said I was depressed.

He started wiping off the countertops with a paper towel. His back was turned to me.

I stood there, my feet on the floor, without moving. A square of light, cast by the window, hung on the refrigerator, the opposite of a shadow, and I could see the heat rising off Carter's car outside the window like a ghost in the light. I could see many things I hadn't seen before, and I closed my eyes.

Maybe it's not that complicated. Maybe Dr. Fontenot told him about our conversation because there was nothing in it he felt he needed to hide, and maybe they're both just concerned about me, and maybe they're right and I'm depressed. I am depressed. I wanted to kill myself last night. I'm not suicidal now, though, and I don't need medication and I won't take it if he brings some for me, but if I do have a mild case of clinical depression, maybe I'll get another kind of glimpse at what it was like to be my mother.

Carter said, "I was concerned about you, and I called him."

Carter put his arms around me, and I buried my face in his chest.

After a while, I loaded the dishes into the dishwasher. My head still hurt. Carter was just standing there by the counter.

I had a dinner plate in my hand, and I stopped and turned and looked at him, and I said, "What do you expect me to do?"

Carter looked at the plate like he thought I was going to throw it. I put it on the counter.

He said, "You mean, on the Zoloft?"

I said, "No. What do you expect me to *do*, with my life?"

I'd told myself I'd work for Audrey until the inauguration, then find something else, something more my own, though I had no idea what.

I was about to cry, and I was using the muscles in my forehead to hold back the tears. I put the plate in the dishwasher. I put in a handful of forks and knives, which made a crashing sound. I was waiting for Carter to answer, wondering what was taking him so long. I put in a wineglass, and I wanted a drink, but I didn't think I should at that hour. I poured myself a second cup of coffee.

Without looking at him, I said, "That wasn't a rhetorical question. I really want to know."

He said, "None of us knows what's next. I'm sure we'll have a strategy meeting next week, and you and Audrey are welcome to come if you want. But we have to stay flexible, keep an open game plan, see what happens."

Fine. I didn't know if he was willfully misunderstanding me or if we just weren't communicating, but I decided to let it drop. Do my part, and my part wasn't over.

I tried to leave it at that. I couldn't think of anything to do *but* leave it at that.

MAYBE I COULD HAVE LEFT IT AT THAT forever.

Maybe I should have.

Because after spending eleven months analyzing every word everyone said or didn't say, every action everyone took or failed to take, every physical detail from the absence of rigor mortis in my mother's eyelids down to the arrangement of the furniture in my father's bedroom, every painful memory from my childhood, and every hint of depression or mania or paranoia in myself and not doing one damn thing about any of it except worry myself sick and stop trusting the people I loved, what finally made me act was the smallest gesture possible, barely a nod.

It was during the Inaugural Ball.

Carter and I got there early, and I was talking to the florist when I saw Dr. Fontenot come in a side door at the other end of the ballroom and hand Carter a small white bag, a pharmacy bag, which I assumed was the Zoloft. He'd been promising to get it all week, but one thing or another had kept delaying him.

When I finished with the florist, Carter brought me the bag and said, "I really think this is going to help you," and I opened it and took out the pill bottle. It was a regular prescription bottle, from a regular pharmacy, the closest one to the Capitol.

He said, "Why don't you go ahead and take one now?"

I said, "I will, when I'm ready."

Carter touched my shoulder—I couldn't tell if it was a gesture of compassion or irritation or pity—and a woman waved to him from across the room, and he said, "I've got to go do this interview. It's live TV."

I said "go," but he was already leaving.

I put the pill bottle in my evening bag.

Why did it take Dr. Fontenot a whole week to call in one prescription?

It stopped me for a moment.

I watched Carter and the reporter go outside.

Then I dismissed the thought and threw away the empty bag. We'd all had a busy week. I'd put things off and left things undone as well.

I looked around for Dr. Fontenot. I wanted to thank him, maybe ask him a question or two about what to expect so I could tell Carter I was having whatever side effects I was supposed to have—but he was gone, too. So I started to follow Carter outside and see if Dr. Fontenot had stepped out, too, but the caterer rushed up to me and grabbed my arm and started explaining some catastrophe involving asparagus and wanting to know if I liked how the buffet table looked. I hated it—he'd carved a hunk of cheese into a map of Louisiana and turned something covered with caviar into an alligator with olives for eyes, and just about everything there was decorated to look like something it wasn't—but it was too late to do anything about it.

I was a little anxious by then, but the caterer was about to hyperventilate, so I didn't read anything into my feelings. Everybody was anxious.

The band was tuning up, and people were starting to arrive.

My father welcomed everyone and danced the first dance alone with Audrey as we all applauded. For the second dance, Carter and I and Dr. and Mrs. Fontenot and Laura and her husband and a few other couples joined in, and for the third, my father cut in on Carter to dance with me, and Carter started dancing with Audrey. Soon everybody who'd contributed to the campaign was dancing. They'd dance past us and pat my father's shoulder and say, "Congratulations, Governor," and he knew them all by name, looked them in the eye and called them by name and thanked them for their support exactly as he'd done eleven months before at the Rex Ball. One or two said, "Next stop, the White House," or, "We'll be with you all the way," and he smiled and said, "I'll need your help," just as he'd said at the Rex while my mother was upstairs, dying.

Time was still racing forward, but something in me had been standing still, and I felt like my past—my mother's past—was catching up with me and repeating itself in me. At the prayer service that morning, I'd kept trying to send up little messages to God, but they'd fall back down, and the air felt thick with the scent of old incense and unanswered prayers. The last time I'd been in church, for my mother's funeral, and the time before that, Ash Wednesday, when I lit a candle for her, I hadn't been able to pray, either, or anytime in between.

Then the walking parade from the cathedral to the Capitol, complete with high-school bands and policemen on horses, felt like walking from the Garden District to the Quarter with Pete Fountain's Half-Fast Walking Club on Fat Tuesday morning, only I couldn't walk—I was wearing new shoes, and my feet were killing me—so halfway through, I got a ride in the back of somebody's truck, which felt like a lame version of a Mardi Gras parade, and in that frame of mind, I heard my father's acceptance speech sounding like the preachers who descend on Jackson Square during Mardi Gras, saying, I know what you need, I know how to make your life better, I offer you hope.

I thought, *There ought to be jugglers and fortune tellers and caricaturists.*

Then I looked around at all the state senators and legislators and journalists and thought, *Close enough.*

And at the ball, of course, my father and Carter and Dr. Fontenot were dressed in their white ties and tails, as they'd been in my mother's suite after she died, and the music and the dancing and the absence of my mother and the undercurrent of anxiety and exhaustion and the sense of an ending that was also a beginning—it all felt strangely like the night my mother died, except that I'd played First Lady at the Rex and Audrey had kept a low profile, while Audrey was First Lady at the inauguration and I was nothing.

My father swirled me around the dance floor, and Audrey swooped past us in the arms of a senator, and I was scanning the room, trying to spot Carter—the last time I'd seen him, he was dancing with Audrey—but I couldn't find him. Then my father spun me around again, and I caught a glimpse of Dr. Fontenot. He was dancing with his wife, but he was looking at me, and when I looked his way, he closed his eyes and turned away, just as he'd done on the veranda when he said, *God forgive us all.*

I was starting to feel dizzy.

When the song the band was playing ended, my father let go of me, and Audrey and the senator were headed our way, and I went to get a drink.

The line at the bar was too long, though, so I went in the ladies' lounge and sat down on the fainting sofa. I opened my purse and got out the pills. I hadn't been planning on taking them, but I was feeling worse—anxious and angry and suspicious—in ways that didn't seem to have anything to do with grief.

I opened the bottle. I didn't know if I needed Zoloft, but I knew I needed something.

I shook one into the palm of my hand and looked at it. I could see it, obviously—it was small and blue—but I couldn't feel it. It was virtually weightless, which felt significant at the time.

I read the label. It had my name on it. Grayson Guillory. My doctor was listed as M. Fontenot. Thirty Zoloft, fifty milligrams each. Everything looked completely normal.

There's nothing here to guarantee that these pills are really Zoloft. They might not even be from Capitol Pharmacy.

The suspicion in my head felt completely unconnected to me, as if I'd just heard somebody else's thought instead of my own.

Why did Dr. Fontenot pick up the pills, but since he did, why not give them directly to me instead of to Carter? And why not just call it in and have me go get them myself, like every other doctor in the world?

I put the pill back in the bottle and put the bottle in my purse.

Maybe he was being nice.

A woman I'd never seen before was freshening her lipstick in the mirror with her back to me, and I looked up at her for no particular reason, and our eyes met in the mirror, and she looked away. She'd been watching me.

I took the bottle back out again and went into a stall and flushed a pill down the toilet.

Just in case Carter counts them to see if I'm taking them. Which wouldn't be like Carter, but just in case.

I still wasn't quite ready to act on what I saw, but I'd turned some kind of corner. And what had changed was not that I suspected Carter, but that I was beginning to trust myself. I could barely hear the nagging little voice in my head that had always told me I was being paranoid.

When I came back into the lounge, the woman wasn't there. She might have had nothing to do with anything, but I was glad she was gone.

I looked in the mirror and forced a glazed-over smile, the smile of the antidepressed.

I should send one of the pills to a lab and ask them what it is, what it's supposed to do to me.

I drew red lipstick on my lips, then kissed a piece of tissue and threw the tissue away.

I could have figured out a way to communicate with a lab without risking Carter finding out I had, but I couldn't come up with a plan of what to do if it was an illegal substance and the lab reported me to the police. I vaguely remembered seeing a paperback in the bookstore that showed what different prescription pills were supposed to look like, but I wouldn't have trusted the picture even if it matched.

I guess I need that drink now.

But when I went out again, Carter was waiting for me at the door, and he was upset.

I said, "What's wrong?"

He said, "Somebody's called in a death threat to your father."

I looked around—there were suddenly plainclothesmen in tuxedos everywhere—and I said, "Who?"

I was scared, but I wasn't panicking. It was a relief, in a mixed-up way, to be facing a danger that I was absolutely certain was not generated by my own brain.

"Probably some crazy King supporter," Carter said. "We don't know. It came from a pay phone about a block from here."

My father was dancing with the woman from the restroom.

I said, "Who's that woman?"

Carter didn't know.

I said, "Why is he dancing with her? What if she's the hit man? What good do bodyguards do if he's dancing?"

Carter held up his hands and said, "I couldn't agree more, but he won't listen to me."

"Then I'll dance with him," I said, and I walked onto the dance floor.

Carter didn't try to stop me.

The woman from the rest room left as soon as I came up to them, and I said, "Who was that?" My father didn't know either.

We started jitterbugging, though I couldn't find his rhythm, and I said, "You have to be more careful. How can you be so calm when somebody wants to kill you?"

He turned me around, then pulled me back close to him.

He said, "I'm wearing a bullet-proof vest."

He held me out at arm's length, then pulled me tight again.

I said, "Well, I'm not, and I'm dancing with you."

I laughed as if it were a joke, but I was terrified.

He said, "Nobody wants to kill you."

He twirled me around under his hand, like a puppet.

To anybody watching, he wasn't letting one hint drop that anything was not going according to plan. It was exactly how he'd acted at the Rex Ball the night my mother died, which had seemed until that moment like evidence of his innocence, but which in the context of the death threat was starting to feel more like evidence of guilt. Except that if he was calm the night my mother died because everything *did* go according to plan, I couldn't figure out for the life of me what the plan for this night was.

Then Dr. and Mrs. Fontenot danced toward us—I could see them over my father's shoulder—and Mrs. Fontenot was in her usual three-martini haze, but Dr. Fontenot winked, either at me or at my father, I couldn't tell, but which he'd never done before, and neither of them said a word to us as they passed by.

I looked in my father's face. He was looking over my shoulder at Dr. Fontenot, giving him the same sly smile I'd seen before, the one that said he knew somebody was keeping his secrets.

It raised a question—set off an alarm, actually—and I tried one last frantic time to explain it away: Dr. Fontenot could know any number of secrets. All doctors keep secrets.

My father pulled me close to him, too close. I was pressed against him.

What if the lights go out and somebody tries to shoot my father but hits me instead, and why isn't he concerned about that?

Carter was nowhere in sight.

Or what if that's the plan? Maybe that's what the smile was about. Maybe they want to kill me, and maybe Dr. Fontenot called in the death threat and my father knows he did, and they know that even if the bullet passes through me to my father, he'll be okay because of his bullet-proof vest, and maybe the Zolofts are really blood-thinners to make sure any wound will make me bleed to death, and the whole thing will look like an accident.

We were still dancing to the same song, but the beat in my brain changed tempos. I couldn't find my own rhythm.

Then my father nodded at Dr. Fontenot.

And that was it. It was the smallest possible nod, barely perceptible, but it connected instantly in my mind to his smile and to Dr. Fontenot's wink and to Earl Long's famous motto.

I looked in my father's eyes. They were ice-blue, like a certain kind of attack dog.

The band kept playing, but I wasn't hearing it. My body kept dancing, but I felt like I was underwater, deep beneath the surface, trying to swim for air but unsure which direction was up.

My father spun me around.

I remembered thinking my mother was paranoid when she thought she was being given the wrong drugs on purpose, and I remembered wishing she was paranoid when she said they wanted to kill her, and I thought, *She was right. If she wasn't right about every last detail, she was still basically right.*

And suddenly I understood the parallel that made all the others make sense: Dr. Fontenot's involvement in my case was exactly what it would have been in my mother's—he'd supplied the drugs—which was exactly what he needed God's forgiveness for, what we all did.

The song was winding down.

It's over now. I've been played for a fool. Dr. Fontenot helped my father and my husband kill my mother, and they all know I know, they know I've known for a long time, and they all think I've been letting them get away with it, because I have.

I knew it the way you know things in dreams, with absolute certainty, because they're true. I knew it in the deepest part of my soul, where I'd always known it and where I'd been lying to myself, and I knew I had to get out of there.

My father's hand was still wrapped around me, touching my back, and the music swirled in the air above us, and the room felt thick and full of static, like just before a storm breaks, and I told him I was thirsty. I pulled myself free.

I crossed the ballroom, my back to my father. The music was getting slower and softer and farther away. Things were falling quickly into place.

He knows I know because Laura told him, and maybe she also told him she convinced me to keep my mouth shut until King was out of the picture, but he's not so sure he can trust me now, which is fair enough, because he can't.

I went to the bar and asked for a vodka with about four drops of pineapple juice, and while I was waiting, Carter found me. The bartender gave me my drink, and Carter asked me if I was okay, and I said I felt sick.

I had no idea how much Carter knew.

He said, "You're just hot, why don't you go outside and get some fresh air."

I said, "Because, for one thing, there's a potential murderer on the loose, and for another thing, I don't need fresh air. I'm sick, and I want to go home."

He said, "Calm down, Grayson. *If* it wasn't just a prank call, *if* the caller was telling the truth—and those are big ifs—but if so, the murderer is probably already inside, so more than likely, you're safer outside than in. Now if you really want to go home, I won't stop you, but I can't take you. This—being here for your father—is my job. But I'll have a state trooper give you a ride."

It made sense.

Maybe he's an innocent here, in the part that involves me. Or maybe not. Maybe he plans to ask a state trooper who's already lined up as a backup in case Plan A failed, and we're going to have a fatal accident.

I said, "I'm picking out my own state trooper, and if you have some kind of problem with that, it's your problem, not mine."

Carter said, through his teeth, "You're being hysterical," and I said, "With good reason," and he scratched his ear and said, "Fine. Anybody you want."

I was so suspicious of everything and everybody at that point that I wondered if the ear scratching was a signal of some kind and a gun was about to go off, but nothing happened.

In the squad car, I took off my shoes, my mother's shoes. I was wearing her pink kid leather pumps from the first inauguration, which had been a pointless, sentimental idea and which were killing my feet. Then I finished my vodka and pineapple juice.

I made the cop walk through the house with me, check every room and every closet. I knew he thought I'd gone crazy, but I couldn't have cared less what he thought or what he told people because as far as I was concerned, the whole world had gone crazy.

Then he left, and I locked the door behind him.

When I passed back through the living room, the fish looked agitated. Carter had bought the wrasse, and the trigger had been harassing it. Carter was hoping they'd work it out between them, but the aquarium wasn't big enough, and there was no place for the wrasse to go, so the trigger was slowly but purposefully killing it. The wrasse was in bad shape, limp and wounded and panting at the top of the tank.

The humane response would have been to take it out and put it in a bowl of salt water in the freezer so it would die quickly and without further pain, but I couldn't do it.

I was mostly quiet inside myself, though a tiny voice in the back of my head was saying, *Maybe you're doing the right thing, or maybe this is just another incidence of a combination of laziness and lack of moral courage, a lifelong habit of living with indecision until it becomes its own decision, doing something by doing nothing.*

I didn't know if I was talking to myself about the wrasse or the Zoloft or the death threat against my father or the fact that I was certain now that my father had killed my mother with drugs provided by Dr. Fontenot, and my husband was primarily responsible for the cover-up, and I had no idea what I was going to do about any of it.

I went in the bedroom and turned on the TV. If the death threat had turned out to be real—if anybody had tried to assassinate my father—it would have happened by then, and it would have been on TV, but it wasn't, and I turned it off.

It was late, and the house felt eerily quiet and angular and unfamiliar-the beginning of a panic attack. I was pretty sure Carter would be out until early morning, smoking cigars. And I knew he'd be up early again the next day for another round of interviews.

I figured I'd need my rest for whatever was ahead of me, so I took two sleeping pills with a glass of wine and went to bed.

T HE NEXT MORNING, CARTER MOANED when his alarm went off. I was wide awake—I'd been lying there for hours, coming up with a plan—but I closed my eyes and pretended to be asleep so I wouldn't have to look at him or listen to him or tell him what I knew.

When he left, I got up and took a fast shower and went to the bank. That same bitch from before was there, but she didn't bother me this time. I just got the tape and the book and closed the safe-deposit box account and left.

I was going to leak the story.

I didn't like it. It was a page borrowed from my father's strategy book—let the media do your dirty work—and I didn't like it being so public and so crude and so far out of my control, how it would unravel, but I was out of other options.

It's this, or let them get away with murder.

I promised myself, *I'm not betraying anybody I love.*

It was a lie, and I knew it, but I couldn't think of a course of action that didn't betray somebody—either my mother, or my father and Carter—so I thought, *At least I'm not betraying the truth.* A cold comfort.

We didn't have the equipment at our house to duplicate the video, and I couldn't take it to a duplicating service because I didn't want anybody to know I had it, and I couldn't go buy a machine to do it because where would I hide it and who would hook it up and figure out how to work it, so I'd resigned myself to handing over the original.

I couldn't do it through the mail, though, because I wanted to do it anonymously but I couldn't insure it or trace it without putting a return address on it, and I couldn't give it to a local TV station because I knew too many people in Baton Rouge—or, rather, too many people knew me—and there was no way to be sure I wouldn't be seen going in or out of the building.

So I drove to New Orleans. I stopped on the way at a drugstore and bought a package of big yellow envelopes and some paper towels and a pre-paid phone card to call home to check for messages without leaving a billing record so I could call Carter right back if he was looking for me, which he wasn't.

My hands were trembling when I wiped my fingerprints off the tape with a paper towel. I debated with myself for a moment over what to do about *Huey Long*—I couldn't keep it, but I could have thrown it away—but I wiped it off and put the video in it, thinking it might have been a piece of evidence that I just hadn't deciphered yet, and I put them both in an envelope. I didn't lick the seal so they couldn't find me through the DNA in my saliva.

I wrapped my hand in a paper towel and wrote SANDY ADAMS on the envelope in big block letters. He was a television reporter in New Orleans who I'd been impressed by during the campaign. I was pretty sure he wouldn't lie, but I was certain he'd walk over his grandmother for this kind of information and wouldn't care if my father knew he was out to get him because everybody already knew he was out to get anybody who could be gotten.

I didn't know what kind of security system the TV station had—whether they used video cameras, for example—so I couldn't just drop it off in person, which meant I needed a disguise, but I couldn't spend all day running around buying a wig and glasses and makeup and clothes and whatever else you can buy to keep yourself from looking like yourself but also to keep from looking like you're wearing a disguise because I had to get back to Baton Rouge before anybody noticed I was gone. So I bought a newspaper to find out what parades were riding that day—Mardi Gras runs from Twelfth Night, January Sixth, to Fat Tuesday, the day before Ash Wednesday, and every krewe has its own parade during that time, and most people who wear costumes before the last four or five days are in the parades. I was going to get a parade costume, but I didn't want to rent anything because of how easy rentals are to trace, so I went to another drugstore and bought a mask of a soul rotting in hell, its face fixed in a scream—it was all they had—and a black robe and a package of beads.

I paid in cash and called home to check for messages again, but there were none, which should have made me feel better, but I felt worse.

I put the costume on over my clothes in the car. Then I dropped off the tape at the station.

I said to the receptionist, "Could you please give this to Sandy Adams?" I didn't disguise my voice because it was just too suspicious on top of the mask.

She said, "Is he expecting it?"

"Not exactly, but I'm sure he'll want to see it."

She smirked.

"What is it in regards to?"

Which was none of her business, and I didn't like where she was going, so I did what my father does to reporters who ask impertinent questions and pretended not to hear her.

I said, "So if you could get it to him as soon as possible, we'd appreciate it."

She said, "Sure."

She wasn't literally shrugging her shoulders, but her voice sounded like she was.

I said, "Thanks."

I had a feeling I hadn't said all I was supposed to say, but I couldn't think of anything else, so I turned to go.

She said, "What krewe are you from?"

"Ulysses."

"Do y'all ride this afternoon?"

"Yeah."

"How is it this year?"

I said, "Not as good as last year," which is what everybody always says about every parade.

She said, "That's what I heard," and I left.

I WANTED TO STAY IN NEW ORLEANS OR maybe go on to Mississippi and try to start a new life there, but I couldn't. Not yet. I didn't want Carter and my father to connect the story breaking with my leaving town and know it was my fault, so I had to keep acting like everything was normal, except I was supposed to be taking the pills, and I didn't know if they were supposed to gradually kill me or make me want to kill myself or cheer me up or just drive me insane. So I thought I'd tell Carter I felt funny and didn't want to talk about it and leave it at that until Sandy Adams came through, which I didn't expect to take long.

But the story didn't break that night. Sandy Adams reported live from a French Quarter balcony—"Behind the iron lace of these beautiful facades lurks a force that threatens to destroy the entire area from the inside out"—but he was talking about Formosa termites. He interviewed an exterminator who said they were getting harder and harder to kill, and he showed a photograph of a massive live oak that had fallen in a storm. It was hollow in the center.

Carter asked about the Zoloft—was I taking it, did I think it was working—but he didn't make an issue of it.

The police caught the guy who'd phoned in the death threat—a teenage prankster.

Nobody was trying to kill my father. Nobody was trying to kill me. Nobody had ever been trying to kill me. Which left me feeling strangely disappointed.

On the morning of the third day, I was walking through the living room, wondering how much longer I could or should wait on Sandy Adams, when I noticed the wrasse was still alive. It looked worse, though, much worse. All its color was gone and it was lying on the bottom. It was clearly suffering, and it was going to die.

I stood there in the middle of the living room, and my mind went blank. I had one of those moments where time seems to have gone on without you and then circled back around to pick you up, and you can't remember if you're coming or going or how or why you got to where you are.

I stood very still, waiting for things to fall back into place.

My heart was pounding in my ears, and I looked at my hands to see if they were trembling, but they weren't. I turned them palms up so my thumbs were on the outside, my pinkies almost touching, and I thought, *My hands look like they were put on backwards.*

My mind wasn't working right—I knew that—and I felt like my body wasn't shaped right.

It's over. I have to let go before I drive myself crazy. My father didn't kill my mother. Carter and Dr. Fontenot didn't help him kill her. I didn't destroy evidence. I have to go on with my life. We all do.

I sat down on the sofa.

I knew I should feel relieved, but I didn't. I was trying to get used to the idea that Sandy Adams had apparently concluded my mother was just a pathetic, paranoid nutcase whose rantings were so pitiful that airing them would have been in significantly worse taste than the blood, guts, and tears they depended on for ratings every day of the week.

No decent reporter would sit on a story like this for three days if he could find anything at all to verify it. So it's not going to air because Sandy Adams couldn't find one piece of evidence or one corroborating witness to convince him it was true, and he couldn't do it for the same reason I couldn't—there wasn't anything, except whatever chemical imbalance was in my mother's head and, later, in mine.

My hands were empty, and I turned them over, palms facing down, and touched the sofa fabric on either side of me.

Okay, it's best this way. This is good. It's time to let go.

I hadn't been trying to be symbolic, waiting three days. I just couldn't stand it any longer, any of it. For months, ever since I'd promised Laura I'd assume my father's innocence, I'd set parts of my life aside—I'd put off thinking about my grief about my mother, my demotion from de facto First Lady to First Lady's Assistant to Nothing, and every other problem I had except the campaign and the inauguration. I was drinking too much and not exercising at all. I wasn't taking birth control, though I wasn't pregnant, and I'd been trying not to think about how rarely we made love, how rarely we talked about anything other than politics, how rarely we laughed.

But for the past three days, I'd been feeling the rest of my life creeping toward me, closing in the way darkness falls when you're lost.

Now I just have to will myself to stop living in fear and start getting on with my life like a normal person. It's that simple. It's what I always thought my mother should have done, and now I have to do it.

I went in the kitchen and wrote a check to pay the electricity bill. I balanced the checkbook, sort of—I hadn't been keeping very good records. I planned menus for the week, went grocery shopping, and came home. While I was putting away the food, I was thinking I should call another couple and invite them for dinner, but I couldn't think of anybody to ask. We didn't have any friends. I hadn't even realized it until that moment. I was rearranging the freezer, trying to make room for a box of peas, when I thought, *If this is the rest of my life, I'm going to go insane. If I'm not already*.

I closed the freezer.

Maybe that's what happened to my mother. She saw the likelihood of her life turning out to be boring and utterly insignificant, and she went crazy instead, and I tried to play political campaigner and female detective for the same reason, but if that's over, now what?

I opened the refrigerator and threw out a jar of old pickles and some salad dressing and a half a jar of spaghetti sauce, all of which had been in that house longer than I had.

Instead of figuring out everybody else's past, I have to start figuring out my own future. Maybe that's why I did what I've been doing for so long, to keep from having to do this.

I threw out some sour milk and wilted cilantro.

I was starting to feel good—out with the old—when I picked up a bottle of champagne we'd been saving longer than I could remember and popped it open. I poured myself a glass—to a new beginning.

By the time Audrey called, later that day, I'd drunk the whole bottle and fallen asleep.

She said, "Why don't you come on over to the Mansion for an early dinner?"

"That's probably fine," I said, "but I'll have to check with Carter."

She said, "He's already here. They just walked in."

I didn't let myself wonder if there was more to the invitation than a simple dinner, didn't ask why she'd invited us, why Carter was there, what anybody's motives were. I just drank a cup of instant coffee, swallowed two Advils with a glass of water, took a fast shower, dressed, and left.

Audrey greeted me at the door—she'd dismissed the staff

early—and brought me upstairs, where Carter and the Fontenots were having cocktails with my father, and offered me a drink.

I said, "Yes, please, white wine," and she went to get it.

Carter whispered, "Are you okay?" which worried me—*why wouldn't I be okay?*—but I said, "I'm fine."

Then I said, "Are you?"

He said, "I guess so."

I said, "What?"

What's wrong?

He said, "I don't know."

Audrey brought my drink, and my father said, "Cheers," and we all repeated him together, "Cheers," the way Baptists say "amen" at church, and we all lifted our glasses and drank at once, the way Presbyterians drink grape juice out of shot glasses in unison during communion.

The thought ran through my mind that we were drinking poison, though I knew we weren't. I'd made a habit of thinking the worst, and I was trying to stop.

I said, "Something smells good."

Mrs. Fontenot stepped out onto the balcony for a cigarette, and Audrey started explaining everything that was wrong with the meal we were about to eat, apologizing in advance for it. She'd cooked it herself. My father and Carter and Dr. Fontenot drifted off together to a corner of the room, ignoring her, which left me to absolve her for the meal, so I said, "I'm sure everything will be fine," and she said, "Famous last words," which she thought was funny.

It was a normal dinner party. I couldn't point to one detail that was out of place. I was trying to convince myself that this was my life now, and it was a good life, but a part of me was feeling like the first time you laugh after somebody you love has died, a combination of relief and guilt and separation from yourself and from the people you love.

They could all die, but eventually, you'd laugh again.

Another part of me was just hungover.

Audrey was still fretting, and I was repeating my assurances to her, saying, "It'll be *fine*," trying to believe myself, when my father walked back toward Audrey and me and said, "Let's see what's on the news," and turned on the TV.

Carter and Dr. Fontenot followed him over to us, and my father motioned for them to have a seat on the sofa in front of the TV. Carter sat down, obedient, and Dr. Fontenot stood beside the sofa, semi-obedient, and my father moved to the chair that formed the short side of an L with the sofa, and Sandy Adams came on the screen.

I froze.

He said, "Our top story tonight, startling new information has emerged about the death of the Governor's late wife. Join us, next."

Audrey said, "Oh my God."

Nobody else said a word.

I looked at my father, who had placed himself where he could see the TV and all our faces. He was looking at Dr. Fontenot, who had been about to light a cigarette.

Then a commercial came on, and Carter looked at my father, as if for an explanation or maybe some instructions, and Dr. Fontenot sat down on the sofa and set his cigarette, still unlit, in an ashtray on the coffee table. Then he put his hand on his forehead, touched his fingers there, as if he wanted to cross himself but thought better of it.

My father didn't turn off the sound, as he usually did during commercials, though he wasn't watching the commercials. He was watching Dr. Fontenot and keeping an eye on Carter. He didn't look at me at all. Nobody did.

I'd finished my wine and I wanted some more, but I was making myself remain calm. Or at least remain perfectly still.

Audrey said, "Oh my God," again, and her eyes seemed to be focusing on something about twelve inches in front of her face, something invisible but terrifying, as if she were trying to look at her own future but couldn't see a thing.

My father said, very calmly, "Audrey, why don't you freshen everyone's drinks."

He knew. He knew this was coming. And Carter knew he knew something, but he didn't know what.

Audrey didn't move.

Because of course Sandy Adams would try to verify it or at least get my father's reaction—why didn't I think of that?—so my father brought us all to the Mansion to watch us watch her so he could see who leaked the information, but he isn't watching me because he doesn't suspect me. He probably didn't even invite me here, that was Audrey's doing. But he doesn't suspect me and he never was trying to kill me because the idea that I would sell him out is as unthinkable to him as the idea that he would kill my mother was at one point to me.

Audrey started shaking her head, and without looking at me, my father said, "Grayson, help Audrey with the drinks"—he wanted to get rid of us—and Audrey stood up and put her hand over her mouth and walked toward the wet bar.

He doesn't suspect me now, but he will.

I wanted to stay and watch him watch them watch my mother, but I followed Audrey. I didn't want to call any attention to myself.

If they were innocent—if we were innocent—the exposure we'd be afraid of now would be the fact that my mother killed herself rather than suffered a heart attack. So if anybody's watching me out of the corner of their eye, that's what they should see me thinking.

Though I couldn't think how to act like I was thinking that.

Behind the bar, Audrey started trembling—she was about to cry—and I put my arms around her, which is what I imagined I would have done if I'd thought the suicide cover-up was about to be exposed. She sunk onto my shoulder, and she whispered, "I'm so sorry. Please believe me, I didn't even know until way after the fact and then I had no choice."

I stepped back, recoiled from her, but before I could react to what she'd said, my mother came on TV.

The screen was split with her picture on the right, and Sandy Adams was on the left, saying, "Tonight, a voice speaks from the grave. New Orleans's Best News Team has come into exclusive possession of a video made by Marie Guillory, the late wife of Governor Tom Guillory, before she died last year. The following edited excerpt from that video includes her own stunning allegations that the Governor himself was plotting to kill her."

Nobody moved a muscle. We were crumbling inside, but we all kept up iron facades. We were each trying not to call attention to ourselves, trying not to reveal what we knew or didn't know or suspected or feared. So we watched the TV, but we were also watching each other out of the corners of our eyes.

Then Sandy Adams was gone, and my mother's face filled the screen, and the phones were already ringing downstairs when she said, "They're trying to kill me."

Audrey picked up her wineglass with an unsteady hand, filled it to the top, took it into her bedroom, and closed the door.

Carter whispered, "Shit," and looked away from the TV, away from all of us.

The upstairs phone rang, then stopped. I assumed Audrey turned off the ringer.

I was watching my father closely for a reaction, but I saw nothing. He was watching Carter and Dr. Fontenot.

Dr. Fontenot couldn't take his eyes off the TV, watching my mother as if he hoped she might offer him some kind of redemptive truth, or forgiveness, or at least an escape plan. He picked up his cigarette, but he didn't light it. He tapped it on his knee, as if it were a tiny gavel.

Mrs. Fontenot stayed outside. As always with her, it was impossible to tell how much she knew of what was happening.

My mother said, "I heard them," and Carter turned back toward the TV, and she said, "I heard their voices through the door. And I'm not talking about hearing voices, I'm talking about *people* who were plotting to kill me."

Dr. Fontenot dropped his cigarette on the floor.

Carter whispered, "Shit," which came out sounding like, Shhhh. Then he finished his drink in one long gulp.

For some reason, I hadn't specifically thought out whose voices my mother had heard—for one thing, I'd been trying to assume she hadn't heard any voices but her own—but the part of me that believed her had been assuming that the voices were my father's and Audrey's, or possibly my father's and Dr. Fontenot's, or all three of them, but I hadn't let myself think that Carter had been in on the actual planning. Only there he was, the man I slept with, the man I'd married, the man I'd thought I loved, acting like he'd been caught, like he knew what my mother had heard when she heard people plotting to kill her because he was there.

I'm an idiot. I'm the world's biggest fool.

My mother said, "A lot of women have ended up dead because they didn't believe their own husband would kill them, but then, of course, he did. And at first I didn't believe it either, I couldn't, because people say things like,'I could just kill her' every day, but nobody means it. Or almost nobody does."

I didn't look at Carter or my father. I looked at my mother, safe behind the glass TV screen. I wanted to be there with her. I wanted to be like her, protected, behind a glass wall. I wanted to be crazy and therefore not responsible for how I'd lived my life, or dead.

My jaw was clenched and my muscles were aching from trying not to move.

She said, "It kills you. It just kills you right there. So you're walking around dead in your body and the rest is just details."

I knew how she felt, in a way I hadn't the first time I heard her say it. I felt dead in the center of me, hollow, and it seemed like it was only a matter of time until that deadness ate its way out to the surface.

I didn't do anything. I stood exactly where I'd been standing when I told Audrey everything would be fine, and I tried to keep watching the TV. My mother disappeared, and Sandy Adams came on the screen with a sad-but-concerned-citizen look on his face—though he'd probably already asked for a raise—and said, "Shocking and disturbing testimony from a troubled former First Lady of Louisiana. The Governor declined our request for a sit-down interview, but we caught up with him at the Capitol for his reaction."

And there was my father, walking up the Capitol steps with Sandy Adams following him, and Sandy said, "Governor, do you have any response to your late wife's claims that you were plotting to kill her?"

My father kept walking and said, "I've not seen any evidence whatsoever that she made such totally absurd accusations, so no, I have no comment."

Sandy said, "We've come into possession of a video she made before she died where she outlines her fears in some detail."

My father put his hand over the camera, and the screen went mostly dark, and his voice kept talking, "What is the meaning of this? Turn off that camera." Then the screen went blank for just a moment—time passed, though it was impossible to say how much—and then the picture was back, and my father was looking straight into the camera, saying, "My late wife, as many of you know, was not well."

Which was true, though also a lie. She was sick, but we'd gone to great lengths to keep the public from knowing about it.

He said, "On occasion, when her mental illness kept her from being able to concentrate well enough to write, she would keep a video diary."

Then he turned to Sandy Adams and said, "And if in fact you have obtained a copy of one of those diaries, the private, intimate, and paranoid rantings of a brave woman in the throes of manic depression whose valiant struggle against her disease was complicated by her deep desire not to fight that battle in the public eye but which was ultimately cut short by a heart attack, I hope you will have the common decency to respect her privacy."

My father disappeared from the screen, and Sandy Adams, back in the studio, said, "New Orleans's Best News Team has reason to believe that Mrs. Guillory's deepest wishes were for the tape to air, and it is out of respect for those wishes that we're doing so."

My father turned off the sound.

The room was silent. The whole house was.

Then he said, "Who's responsible for this?"

On TV, another reporter stood in front of Dr. Fontenot's office door, looking perky but concerned.

My father was looking at Dr. Fontenot, who was looking at the floor, shaking his head, as if to deny responsibility but accept it at the same time by expressing his regret.

Dr. Fontenot crossed himself.

Nobody said a word. If I didn't know better, I would have thought Dr. Fontenot had just confessed to turning over the tape.

My father and Carter seemed to come to the same conclusion. Carter said, "Fuck, Mike. What in the hell were you thinking?"

Dr. Fontenot said, "Me? You think I—"

Carter interrupted him. "If you wanted to destroy yourself, I'd give you the gun to do it, but why'd you have to bring everybody else down with you?"

My father touched Carter on the elbow. Carter stopped talking and walked over to a window.

My father picked up a phone, dialed an in-house extension, and said, "Take Grayson home."

Dr. Fontenot was walking over to Carter saying, "You think it was my fault?" He wasn't angry or defensive. He just seemed to have lost his capacity to understand what was happening.

"I'm not going anywhere," I said.

Nobody was listening to me.

I went to Carter, tapped his shoulder, but he waved me away, and a state trooper appeared in the doorway—he must have been waiting in the hall—and said, "Are you ready to go, Ms. Guillory?"

"No, I'm staying here," I said.

My father said to the cop, "No she's not," and then to Carter, "Don't use that," meaning the cell phone, which Carter had just taken out of his pocket, though I couldn't imagine who he'd be trying to call.

My father wasn't looking at me, the way a jury won't look at a defendant they're about to find guilty. Nobody was looking at me except the cop.

I said, "I'm not leaving."

My father said to the state trooper, "Go," and he indicated with a gesture of his hand that the trooper was supposed to take me with him, and the trooper touched my arm in a way that said he would grab me if I resisted.

I said, "Carter!" but he pretended not to hear me.

The cop hadn't let go of my arm, and the news, which had gone to a commercial, came back on, but they started another story.

It was clear that Carter hadn't turned over the tape, and it was about to become clear that Dr. Fontenot hadn't, though Carter and my father still thought he had, and it suddenly occurred to me that I should get out of there before my father started looking for another suspect, so I said, "All right, I'm coming," and jerked myself out of the state trooper's grip and got my purse.

The phones were ringing, but nobody was answering them.

Carter was pacing back and forth in front of the TV, my father was pouring himself a drink, Dr. Fontenot was hunched over on the sofa, and Mrs. Fontenot was still out on the balcony, smoking, when I left.

In the car, the police radio was on, but I couldn't understand what the people on it were talking about, couldn't make out their words through the static. We passed two news vans, headed toward the Mansion, though they wouldn't get in.

The trooper said nothing to me the whole way home.

I didn't say anything to him either. I was trying not to scream or burst into tears or confess to turning over the tape.

When we got there, he got out with me and walked me to the door and waited while I unlocked it. Our phone was ringing, but I didn't answer it.

I wanted the cop to leave, but he came inside and looked around. He looked in the closets, under the bed, in the shower, the way my father used to do when I was a child, afraid to go to sleep. Then he'd say, "Not a monster in the house," and he'd turn out my lights.

I didn't know who or what the cop was looking for, but by the time he was ready to go, I was scared of whatever it was, and I wanted him to stay, but he left.

Then I went in the living room and turned on the TV to the station where Sandy Adams worked. They were doing the weather.

I turned off the TV and called the Mansion, five different Mansion phone numbers including Audrey's private line and Carter's cell phone, and they were all busy, or off the hook. I didn't know what I would have said if I'd gotten through, but I wanted to take the temperature over there.

I tried to picture myself doing something reasonable and constructive, but I couldn't think of anything reasonable or constructive to do. I paced around the house for a while thinking, *What the hell, what in the hell, what in hell.*

I went outside for some fresh air.

This was exactly what I wanted, what I deliberately set in motion. If they were guilty, I had to know it, prove it, make sure they wouldn't get away with it. So what in hell is wrong with me, feeling like I had no idea it was coming and it's not what I wanted at all?

I still had my keys in my hand. I hadn't put them down since I unlocked the door.

My mistake was, I didn't have a plan. Plan A was that I wouldn't need a plan because the video would never air because my father was innocent, but we've moved on to Plan B now, so I have to figure out what the fuck Plan B is.

I got in the car and started driving, just driving around.

Maybe I'll go kill my father. Maybe I'll walk in his office and get his hunting rifle off the wall and tell him I'm going to kill him and he won't believe me because he thinks I'm crazy. He won't even be scared. Then I'll shoot him in the heart, one shot, barely any blood shed, and he'll fall down on his knees, and for one bright moment he'll know he underestimated me and my mother, he'll know we didn't let him get away with murder, and then he'll die.

I let the idea sit inside me for a moment, calming me, like smoke that you keep in your lungs before you exhale. Of course I knew I wouldn't kill my father, couldn't watch him die. I took a deep breath and held it and exhaled, very slowly.

I have to figure out where I'm going.

I didn't want to go to a bar.

I did want to go to a bar, actually, and get plastered, but I knew it was a bad idea.

I pulled into a gas station to get some gas.

Maybe I'll just leave now, leave town, leave Louisiana, leave the country and not come back. I shouldn't have come back from New Orleans in the first place.

I was standing there pumping gas, trying to decide where to go.

I can't leave now. For one thing, they'd know I'd turned over the video and they'd find me, and I don't know exactly what they'd do, but I know they'd do something. They couldn't let me get away with it. My father never lets anybody get away with anything. And two, if Sandy can't prove they did it, I'd be coming this far just to let them get away with murder, literally, and

I've always let everybody get away with everything, but that's about to change.

I paid for the gas and left. Then I drove around some more, trying to calm down, get a sense of direction. I was sort of lost.

By the time I got home, I was in the kind of electric calm that comes before a storm. It was late, but Carter wasn't there, though I could tell he had been. A broken glass lay in pieces on the kitchen floor. It was shattered, as if it had been thrown rather than simply dropped, though it was hard to imagine Carter in his starched shirt throwing glassware. I was trying to get used to the idea that Carter was capable of doing lots of things I couldn't exactly imagine him doing.

I'd been there before, to the glass-breaking stage, with Ray. I hadn't particularly wanted or expected to get back to it with Carter, but there we were.

It's all over but the end.

I looked at the clock on the stove. It was 2:53 A.M.

I went in the living room and stood in the window, looked out at the empty street. The streetlights were on, but all the house lights were off. All our neighbors were sleeping. A car drove by.

I wasn't waiting for anything in particular. I wasn't waiting for anything at all. I just had no earthly idea what to do next, where my life was going to go from there, where any of our lives would go, so I stood there at the window, looking at my own reflection in the glass as much as anything. Another car drove by slowly. I didn't normally look out the window at three in the morning, but it struck me as odd.

It was dark outside, and I was suddenly afraid of the dark, and I stepped away from the window and closed the curtains. I walked through the house, closing all the curtains, locking all the doors.

When I passed through the den, I noticed a note that was taped to the aquarium: "I'm sorry," it said, in Carter's handwriting. "It was my fault."

The wrasse was gone. I'd told him not to get that fish, known it would end up dead. Though I could think of a few other things that were also his fault.

The trigger that had killed the wrasse was swimming around as if nothing had happened. I didn't know if the wrasse was in the freezer or the garbage can, but I didn't want to look. I wanted to forget about it. It was time to start forgetting.

I went in the kitchen and got out a glass, an old-fashioned, and poured enough licorice liqueur to cover the bottom. The liqueur smelled sweet, like fire, better than real licorice. If Carter had been there, he would have chilled the glass first, then he'd toss it in the air, spinning it, to line it with liqueur. But I didn't want to break it—too much was falling through my fingers already—so I swirled it around in my hand. I measured a shot of rye whiskey, then poured it into the glass. It smelled wet and ancient and warm, like a fermented ocean.

I was trying not to wonder where Carter was, what he was doing or thinking or feeling. He was out of my life, I knew that.

I added half a shot glass of sugar water and three ice cubes, then four dashes each of Peychaud's and Angostura bitters.

The first time Carter made me a Sazerac, he explained every step, the spinning, the measuring, the pouring. It was a ritual for him. When he got to the bitters, he held up his glass and said, "Life is a Sazerac. It's the two kinds of bitters that give it its flavor."

I said, "What are the two kinds?"

I was playing into his hands on purpose. I was falling in love with him, or I thought I was.

He shook four dashes out of the first bottle into each glass and said, "Not getting what you want." Then he shook four drops from the other bottle. He said, "And getting it."

Later that night, we made love for the first time.

And in my memory, the tastes of whiskey and bitters and sugar water and licorice and Carter's skin and his mouth and his sweat—it was all one thing. It was what I wanted, or what I'd thought I wanted, and not what I wanted at all.

I shaved a piece of lime peel onto the counter and dropped it into the glass the way Carter taught me, twisting it, to release the zest.

I said out loud, "This is for you, Carter."

I drank it carefully at first, trying to taste all the flavors at once and trying to remember the way Carter's breath used to taste in my mouth. Then I tried to remember all the things we'd toasted the night I moved in with him, when everything we wanted was ahead of us, there for the taking, but I couldn't think of any of them. I drank the rest of it meditatively, sucking it down, trying to forget.

Carter didn't come home that night.

The next morning, Dr. Fontenot was found dead from what the TV news reported was an accident. An experienced hunter, he'd supposedly been cleaning his rifle when he shot himself in the head.

I called Carter's cell phone. No answer. I called it again and again.

I stayed in the house all day, waiting for Carter. The phone kept ringing—mostly reporters, though at least once it was Audrey—but I let the machine get it. No word from my father.

That afternoon, the doorbell rang. I looked through the peephole and saw two state troopers from the Mansion, the one who'd driven me home the night before, and another one, and I knew from their faces that something had happened, something bad, something involving Carter.

No, it's about Dr. Fontenot, they're here to tell me he's dead. Please let it be that.

I opened the door and said, "Come inside." I couldn't think of their names. I knew that my father's physician dying in a hunting accident wouldn't result in state troopers coming to my house.

They followed me into the living room without saying a word. They were wearing guns.

I said, "Have a seat. Would you like some coffee, a soft drink?"

Whatever they had to say, I didn't want to hear it.

They didn't want the coffee, but they appreciated the offer. We were all being excruciatingly polite.

The one who'd driven me home before suggested that I might like to sit down, but I said, "No. I'd rather stand."

He took a deep breath and said, "Ms. Guillory, there's no easy way to say this. Your husband was in an accident last night."

I said, "No."

I sat on the sofa.

I wasn't in denial. I knew it was true, and I knew he was dead. I was trembling—I held onto my knees to keep my hands under control—but I was calm.

He was murdered. My father murdered him, or had him murdered, which is the same thing. Same with Dr. Fontenot. I could be next.

I said, "How?"

The cop said, "He drove halfway over the Mississippi on I-10, stopped to fix a flat tire, and, apparently, he . . . fell off. His car was found on the bridge, and his body washed up on the shore about an hour ago."

Carter had never fixed a flat tire in his life.

He didn't fall.

He didn't jump either, which was what the cop seemed to think.

He was pushed.

And whoever did it left the car on the bridge and punctured his tire as a cover.

I started crying, trying not to, though at least as much from fear as from grief.

He said, "Can we do anything for you?"

It struck me as a ridiculous question. What could anybody possibly do?

I said, "No."

Then I said, "But thank you."

His hand jerked toward my shoulder. He wanted to touch me, comfort me, but he was afraid to.

The other cop was just looking around the room, as if my husband being dead embarrassed him.

The first one said, "You going to be okay?"

How am I supposed to answer a question like that?

I shook my head yes, but I didn't say anything.

The cop who hadn't opened his mouth yet said, "Ms. Guillory, we don't want to impose, but would you mind if we took a look in your husband's study?"

"Why?"

He didn't have an instant answer. He looked at his partner.

The partner said, "We just want to make sure there aren't any sensitive documents. And if he'd brought some files of ongoing projects home to work on them, of course, the Governor's office will need them back."

I knew something was wrong, but I also knew they wouldn't find anything incriminating there. I'd looked before.

I was still trying to absorb the shock. Plus, I didn't see where I had a choice. So I said, "Go ahead."

I waited in the living room, in front of the fish. I didn't call anybody. I didn't say anything. I just sat there. I had no idea for how long.

By the time they were done, my hands were shaking. I didn't think I was doing anything else out of the ordinary, but the cop who'd driven me home before said, "Ms. Guillory, you really need to calm down. Would you like a glass of water?"

I said, "No."

He said, "Come in the kitchen. Show me where the glasses are." I followed him in, gave him a glass.

The other cop was carrying boxes out, box after box.

The first one filled his glass with tap water and said, "Why don't you come with us to the Mansion?"

"No. I want to stay here."

They didn't want to leave without me. I thought they might kidnap me, but they didn't.

I said, "I just need a little time alone first."

I walked them to the door and opened it for them.

"Are you sure you don't want to come? Maybe you shouldn't be alone right now."

I said, "I'm sure."

He put the glass of water on the counter.

After they left, I poured myself a glass of wine and sat down on the sofa, facing the fish. The Picasso kept picking up mouthfuls of sand and spitting them out at the other end of the tank, claiming a new territory. The other fish were staying out of his way.

I walked over to the tank to take a look at them.

Carter's note about the wrasse was gone.

I bent down and looked for it on the floor, behind the curtains.

The state troopers had taken Carter's note without asking for an explanation. It had said, "I'm sorry. It was my fault," which could be wildly misconstrued. I'd said they could have government files, but I never gave them permission to take my personal property.

I ran outside—I was going to stop them, I wanted it back—but their car was already gone.

Lying thieves.

When I came back inside, the phone was ringing, but I let the machine get it. It was my father. He wanted to talk to me. I was supposed to call him when I got in, and he'd come right over.

Apparently, I'm not being watched, or he'd know I'm here. Though if the house was bugged, somebody might have figured I left when I went outside.

I was being very quiet.

Audrey called, and the machine got it. She'd heard the news about Carter and was heartbroken for me. Did I want her to come over?

A reporter from the Baton Rouge *Advocate* gave me his condolences and his pager number.

Carter's mother called from New Orleans. She would handle the funeral arrangements if that would take the burden off me. I picked up the phone.

I said, "Hi, it's me."

She said, "Grayson, are you okay?"

I said, "Yeah. Are you?"

"Well, I'm . . . no. But do you want me to make the arrangements?"

"Oh. I haven't gotten that far."

"Let me handle this. It would be a comfort to me."

"Okay. Thank you."

"I'm thinking we should have a requiem mass at the Cathedral in Baton Rouge, and your father has offered to host the wake at the Mansion, and then we'll bring him home to our family vault. I think he would have wanted it that way."

How is it that a person who had no idea what he wanted before he died suddenly knows exactly what he would have wanted if he were still alive? Though how could he have wanted a requiem mass and a burial in the family vault without also being dead?

I knew it was an inappropriate response, but the whole thing— the mass, the wake, the burial—none of it seemed appropriate. Carter's death wasn't appropriate.

I said, "Okay."

I couldn't tell what she was feeling, except that she wanted her agnostic son to be buried as a Catholic.

So this is what it feels like to plan your husband's funeral.

I didn't feel anything. I felt numb.

She said, "I was thinking day after tomorrow? Around one o'clock?" She sounded like she was planning a lunch date.

"Okay."

I couldn't think this way—times and dates and places. I was in a part of my brain where time is fluid, where Carter was still alive and I hadn't taken the actions that led to his death.

She said, "That's Mardi Gras day, you know."

"No. I mean, yes, I know. But I didn't think of it."

I was having trouble processing very basic information.

"But we can't do it tomorrow. That's too soon, there's not enough time to make the arrangements, and the church isn't available on Ash Wednesday because they're having services all day, and I think waiting until Thursday is just too long, don't you think?"

"I guess."

"So what choice do we have?"

"I don't know."

I didn't see that I had much choice about anything at that point. I'd already made all my choices.

"So if it's at one, people who have to get back to New Orleans for Rex have time. Of course, we won't go this year."

"No."

"But you have to think of these things."

I said, "Of course."

She said, "Honey, we've got six reporters on our front lawn, what's it like where you are?"

"I don't know. I closed the curtains."

"Well, that's good. You keep them closed."

"Okay."

She said, "I think that's a very good idea."

Carter's mother and I had never been particularly close, but I felt something tender for her. And I thought I should explain to her about the note before she heard it on the news, but I didn't know how to tell her about that without explaining everything else.

I said, "You didn't deserve this."

Then, all of a sudden, she was crying hard.

When the phone rang again, I didn't answer it. It was my father. We had to talk. It was urgent, no matter how late I got in.

Three newspaper reporters and Sandy Adams called. Somebody claiming to be from *The New York Times*.

During the five-o'clock news, I packed a suitcase.

The local station reported that Dr. Fontenot's death was being investigated with suspicions of foul play, that Carter had been found dead after leaving a suicide note in which he apologized for an unnamed offense and that his wife, the Governor's daughter, was currently under sedation.

My father was behind it. The state troopers had told him everything—they'd come here looking for something to incriminate Carter with, probably something specific my father had arranged for earlier, but they'd hit some kind of jackpot when they found the note about the wrasse.

I let that thought sit heavy in my stomach. I couldn't digest it.

Anybody who puts two and two together will think they have four.

I got my mother's gun out of the velvet boot and put it in my purse.

When the news was over, my father called again. He said, "Grayson, are you there?" Then louder, "Are you there? I know you're there. Now pick up the phone."

I didn't know what he wanted, but whatever it was, I was certain I didn't want to give it to him.

I left the lights on in the house.

Several reporters were waiting in the yard. They photographed me asking them to leave me alone.

I SPENT TWO DAYS DRINKING, WATCHING TV, ordering room service, and crying in a hotel in St. Francisville, where I'd checked in under a fake name.

On the day of the funeral, I drove straight to the Cathedral in Baton Rouge, not stopping by home first. I got there early—I didn't know if there'd be parade traffic because of Mardi Gras, but there wasn't. A mob of reporters had already lined up outside, though, with cops keeping them out of the church, and I lowered my head as I walked up the stairs. It was a sunny day, but their cameras were flashing like warning lights.

Inside, I let total strangers hug me and kiss me and pray over me. I wasn't feeling much. I was thirsty. Other than that, though, I didn't feel anything.

My father was already there, and by the time I spotted him, he was walking toward me. The people between us were clearing a path for him, like he was God. Everybody had stopped talking when my father started coming toward me—nobody was moving or making a noise—and an organ was playing something that sounded like ghosts, so I listened to the only sound I could hear, my father's shoes on the stone floor, first one, then the other, one, then the other, like a clock ticking down.

I looked at his face, the face of the man responsible for the deaths of my mother and my husband. There was a stained-glass window behind him, as if he were emanating light, and I couldn't see his features well. I barely recognized him.

I'd spent the past forty-eight hours demonizing him, teaching myself to think of him as nothing but a cold-blooded murderer who would kill anybody, including me, who got in his way. But there he was, the only real family I had left in the world, standing in front of me looking exhausted and fragile and genuinely grief-stricken.

This is what it means to be heartbroken. My heart is broken into two parts, one that wants him to hold me, and one that's afraid he'll kill me.

When he got to me, he put his arm around me, rested his hand on my shoulder. His hand felt cold. He said, "We need to talk." He whispered it in my ear, and his breath was hot.

Anybody looking at us—everybody there was looking at us—and anybody would have thought he was trying to comfort me.

I said, "*I* don't need to talk." It was the first time in my life I could remember telling him no.

He touched my elbow and said, "Let's take a walk down the hall."

As if I hadn't said a word.

I didn't want to be alone with him, especially not in an unfamiliar building. I didn't really think he'd kill me, not in a church during Carter's requiem mass, but I didn't completely trust him not to, either. Anything seemed possible. And I didn't want to talk to him again, ever, about anything.

I said, "There are people everywhere, and the service is about to start."

The press had been told to stay outside, but a reporter I recognized from the campaign was hovering nearby, posing as a mourner. My father glanced at her.

He said, "We'll have to put this off until the wake."

"Fine."

"Don't do any media before then."

"I'm not talking to the media. I'm not talking to anybody."

I meant I wasn't going to talk to him, but he didn't hear it.

He said, "Good."

During the service, we were all just going through the motions. Anybody who knew Carter knew he wasn't a believer, not in anything but my father.

We said the Twenty-third Psalm together—"I shall not want"— and I thought, *That's a third kind of bitter, not wanting anything, not even wanting to want, because you know all desire brings pain.*

We said, "I will fear no evil," and I thought, *But what if evil runs in your blood? Shouldn't you fear that? Doesn't the real danger lie in not fearing evil?*

I didn't even try to come up with answers to my questions. I didn't want to know the answers.

At the wake, I tried to avoid my father. People I'd never seen before were weeping. Maybe they were Carter's relatives, though I didn't know them. I kept thinking, *They're coming out of the woodwork, like Formosa termites.* For a long while, I sat in the front parlor with a priest who tried to convince me that God would comfort my pain and that Carter was in heaven. I wanted to believe him, but I didn't think he believed himself. Nothing felt true. I knew, intellectually, that Carter was dead, but even that didn't feel true.

If there is a heaven, surely Carter's not there.

I was trying not to think about where he was, if he was anywhere. I'd spent the past forty-eight hours thinking, which hadn't gotten me anywhere, and I was trying to stop.

My father touched my elbow and I jumped—he'd approached

me from behind, startled me—and he asked me to come upstairs with him.

I said, "I'm talking to Father McNally right now."

The priest said, "No, we're finished. You be with your family now." He stood up and shook my father's hand. "Good to see you, Governor."

I said, "Let me get something to drink first."

I was going to leave.

He said, "I'll give you a drink upstairs."

The priest said, "Take some time with your father. Go."

Whatever this is, get it over with.

I said, "Okay."

There were two staircases that lead upstairs—a private one off the kitchen, and one in the main public area that circled around a State of Louisiana seal made out of marble on the floor, which we almost never used. He led me up that one so people would see us go, and I followed, staring at his shiny shoes—one of the murderers on staff always kept my father's shoes shined—and I remembered a moment from my childhood. He was teaching me to water-ski, and he put his feet in the rubber shoes on the skis, and I stood, barefoot, in front of him, leaning back against him, and we held on to the rope together, my hands in the middle, his on the outside, and he said, "Relax, let it happen," and the boat pulled us up and we were gliding over the surface of the lake like Jesus walking on water. I thought my father could do anything.

When we got in the living room, he went to the bar and picked up a corkscrew. I knew he wasn't going to try to kill me with it, but I also knew he could.

Still, there's nothing he can't do.

I sat down on the sofa in front of the TV, and he uncorked a bottle of red wine. He poured me a glass and sat down beside me.

I didn't drink it.

He hadn't poured any for himself.

It was very quiet. We were both looking forward, at the TV, which wasn't on.

I was thinking about skiing, the way my arms ached afterward and my legs wobbled and my skin felt tight with sunburn.

He touched my hand, and I pulled away.

After a long silence, he said, "Look, I know what you think."

I said, "I don't even know what I think."

He said, "I didn't kill your mother."

I turned toward him, and he looked me straight in the eye and said, "You have to believe that."

I'd spent the past two days imagining this moment. I'd been putting us in the kitchen for some reason, and he'd tell me he didn't do it, not so much to convince me he was innocent but to convince himself that I was going to let him get away with it, and I'd pull out a knife and stab him in the heart. Then I'd sit there with him on the floor, holding him, until he died in my arms. Sometimes, his dying words were, "I love you." Sometimes they were, "I'm sorry." Sometimes they were, "Oh my God." But always, he died, and he always knew I'd killed him.

I couldn't do it, though. I couldn't kill him for the same reason I knew he couldn't kill me. I was his daughter. We were family. We needed each other.

I said, "Okay."

"Okay what?"

"I'll believe you."

I was lying. I knew I had to confront him, but this wasn't the time for that.

I took a sip of wine, then set my glass on the coffee table. My hands felt wobbly.

I started crying, and he put his arms around me, and I put my head on his shoulder and cried and cried and he held me tight.

After a while, I started to quiet down. I started feeling like I'd never want anything again, which felt safe.

My father said, "Carter was a good man."

I stood up.

I said, "Don't." Meaning, Don't play me for a fool.

He didn't ask, Don't what? He didn't acknowledge I said it. But he'd heard me.

He stiffened his neck. He looked at his watch, though it didn't matter what time it was.

He said, "We should get back."

I led the way down the front stairs, him following so close behind I felt he was chasing me. I didn't like being in front of him, where I couldn't see him. He was touching my back. I didn't like that either.

I went into the ladies' room to compose myself and closed the door.

That's what I have to do—compose myself. Write a new life for myself, a new identity, make it up.

I washed my face. I'd worn waterproof mascara, but I still had black smudges under my eyes, and I rubbed them off.

When I came out, I didn't see my father. People I'd never laid eyes on were standing around the buffet table, eating fried chicken and little meat sandwiches on white bread cut into triangles and canapés topped with crawfish like there was no tomorrow. All the women had on diamond rings. I couldn't explain, even to myself, why that bothered me as much as it did.

I went in the front parlor, where I saw my father's back. I didn't want to be with him, but I wanted to know where he was. He was talking to Carter's father, and I edged closer to them, and he said, "She still hadn't recovered from her mother's death when this happened. And of course she'd always had her mother's genes. So I can't help but fear for her mental health."

I said, "I'm not going insane."

He couldn't have known I was behind him, but he acted like he wasn't surprised to see me, which is how he always responded to unexpected bad news.

He said, "Of course you're not, sweetheart."

He'd never called me sweetheart in his life.

He said, "I'm just voicing my concern for you."

He touched my shoulder, just barely pressed it, but he didn't smile. Not that he should have smiled at my husband's wake. But there was something about the way he said it, patronizingly, like the fact that I'd denied I was crazy only proved I was.

I walked away, and I had a feeling he was exchanging meaningful looks with Carter's father.

Fuck him.

I was hungry and ashamed of myself for letting him get to me and ashamed of myself for being hungry.

Audrey brought me a plate of food and told me I had to eat, sounding like a mother, and I took it in the kitchen.

Luther was there, spreading cream cheese and smoked salmon on water crackers, arranging them on a tray. He didn't look up when I came in.

I said, "Hi."

He said, "Hey."

I sat down.

He offered me a cracker. He said in a low voice, "I sure am sorry."

I said, "Thanks," and ate the cracker.

He said, "You holding up okay?"

"I guess. I don't know."

He brought me a bottle of Coke from the refrigerator, and I pressed the cold glass against my forehead. Luther's tray was full, and he picked it up and said, "I'll be right back."

I had an urge to follow him out there and tell my father with all those people there as my witnesses that I was not crazy and that if he tried to have me committed to an insane asylum, I would expose him for who he really was and the real reasons Carter was dead.

But I talked myself out of it. I was going to expose my father—or the media would, surely, and I'd be there for it—but Carter's wake wasn't the time or place, and that wasn't the way. For one thing, he'd use whatever I said against me to make the case that I was out of touch with reality because of excessive grief and therefore a danger to myself, and he'd just have me locked up sooner.

I drank my Coke.

I wasn't making a plan. I was just trying to get through the day.

When Luther came back, he said, "I know the timing's awkward, but this might be goodbye. I just wanted you to know. The parole board said yes this time."

I said, "That's wonderful, Luther."

I felt like crying.

I looked out the window, and I saw Audrey step out the side door and light a cigarette, though she didn't usually smoke. A reporter I recognized from the *Times-Picayune* met her there instantly, as if the meeting was planned.

Audrey glanced over her shoulder.

I said, "I'm happy for you. I just . . . well, you're right, though, about the timing. I'm sorry."

I meant I couldn't talk about it just then, couldn't celebrate. Audrey was talking fast, and the reporter was taking down what she was saying in a little spiral-topped notebook. He kept nodding in agreement with her.

Luther said, "I know," and got out two loaves of French bread and started slicing them on an angle with a bread knife.

I walked out the kitchen door and around the side of the house and stood behind a column to listen.

I heard Audrey say, "We're going to get her the help she needs. The best of everything. It's an illness, you know, and we're just going to have to educate the public so hopefully she won't suffer from the stigma of it like her mother did."

The reporter said, "Thank you so much."

Audrey said, "Glad to be of help."

Then she shook the reporter's hand, dropped her cigarette on the ground and put it out with her foot, and slipped back inside.

I leaned against the column.

They won't kill me if they can get away with having me institutionalized, where anything I said they did would be heard as the rantings of a grief-stricken lunatic. And they will get away with it, just like they'll get away with murdering my mother, and a lot of people know it. My father, Audrey, probably Carter's father, probably a few state troopers and a doctor or two, though with Dr. Fontenot gone, it might take them half an hour to find another crooked physician.

I should be terrified. Any rational person would be.

But I wasn't. I was dead calm.

I went back inside. I walked around saying hello to people, thanking them for coming, trying to appear extremely sane, which felt sort of crazy.

I WENT STRAIGHT FROM THE WAKE TO THE Capitol and into the elevator. I passed my father's floor and Carter's and Laura's and the attorney general's three floors and got out at the top. Then I took a small elevator to the roof and went outside, alone.

I wasn't going to kill myself, though the thought occurred that if I did, if I jumped, my father would have to walk over the spot where I died every day on his way to work. It wasn't a revenge fantasy. It was more like a realization that it could happen, and he'd do it, walk right over it. He could live with that.

I'd come there trying to see The Big Picture, put things in perspective, and I thought, *Apparently it's working*.

I could see the bridge over the Mississippi where Carter died and a barge moving under it and the oil refineries and a long chain of railroad cars and the suburbs of Baton Rouge so thick with trees they looked like forests, like hunting grounds. I couldn't see any people at all.

I was saying goodbye.

I drove to the Fontenot estate on my way out of town. It was just after three o'clock in the afternoon, and Mrs. Fontenot answered the door with a martini in one hand and a cigarette in the other. She was wearing some sort of housecoat, with brightly colored layers of silk flowing everywhere. She didn't look surprised to see me. I didn't think much of anything would have surprised her, in her condition.

I said, "Mrs. Fontenot, could I come in?"

She said, "If you want. I'm not exactly fit for company, though."

She turned around and walked over a zebra skin rug, through her foyer, into the living room, and I went in and closed the door behind me. There were dead animals everywhere—rams' heads on the walls, a bear skin rug on the floor, a deer-antler chandelier on the ceiling, a wastebasket made from an elephant's foot.

I said, "I'm so sorry about your husband."

She said, "I'm sorry about yours."

She tapped her cigarette ashes into the palm of an ashtray that looked like a gorilla's hand and offered me a cigarette.

I said, "No. Thank you."

I thought the ashtray had to be fake, but I wasn't sure of anything anymore. She was wearing a diamond as big as a kumquat on her hand, which I'd always assumed was real, but you never know. The boundary between real and fake was starting to fade. All kinds of boundaries were fading. I wished I hadn't come.

The only living animals in the room were fish. She had seven round, crystal bowls on her mantel over the fireplace, six of which each held a single Chinese fighting fish. They're the most beautiful freshwater fish there is, colorful, with long, flowing fins that reminded me of Mrs. Fontenot's outfit. They're generally peaceful with other kinds of fish, but they'll fight to the death if they're put in the same tank with their own species. The last bowl in the row was full of ashes.

She said, "I still haven't washed my hands. I just put them in there. They give them to you in a plastic bag, like it's garbage, so I was transferring them into a bowl. But I don't know what to do with that—whoever it is."

Her hands were sooty. She rubbed them together, letting the dust fall to the floor.

I said, "What to do about what?"

"They gave me the wrong ashes."

As gently as I could, I said, "How can you tell?"

She put her hand in the bowl and picked two small pieces of metal off the top. She held them out to me on the palm of her hand.

She said, "Have you ever seen anything like this before?"

I said, "No."

She said, "It's a bullet." As if that explained everything.

I said, "Oh."

I picked one up and looked at it. It was a little scrap of metal.

"I'm sorry, Mrs. Fontenot. Maybe . . . I don't know what shrapnel looks like, but was he ever in a war?"

I gave it back to her.

"These are not from the war," she said.

Gently, I said, "Maybe not, but they're not bullets. I'm sorry."

"Of course it's not bullets." She hissed the *S*. "It's one bullet. Or part of one. There would have been five or six pieces, but the coroner kept the rest, apparently thinking he had the whole thing, incompetent asshole."

The coroner. "His brother?"

"No. That's my point. His brother would have known this wasn't Mike's bullet. So it had to be some other coroner with some other body from some other place."

I said, "Dr. Fontenot's brother did his autopsy?"

"Well, that's his job, darling."

Just when you think you've heard everything.

"Which is how I know this is not my husband," she said.

"I'm sorry," I said. "I'm lost."

"This bullet is frangible."

I didn't know what that meant. I just looked at her.

"Frangible bullets shatter on impact," she said.

I said, "I didn't know there was such a thing."

She went on, "They kill anything, but they do too much damage. Mike always tried to leave his kills intact so he could mount them. He was very careful about that. And they're illegal, though of course a person who wants them badly enough can get them. But my husband would never have used them. Never."

There it was, physical evidence.

At least it was physical evidence that he'd been murdered instead of accidentally killed himself. I hadn't held physical evidence of anything I suspected since I crushed my mother's pill bottles into fragments and threw them away, but here I was, looking at a piece of the bullet that killed Dr. Fontenot, the bullet that murdered him.

She said, "I've been around guns and ammunitions all my life, and I know this is not the bullet that was in my husband's hunting rifle. So you tell me, how did it end up in these ashes, unless these are somebody else's?"

She put both pieces back in the bowl of ashes and wiped her hands on her hem.

I didn't answer her. I didn't know how much to say, how much to trust her, how much she could handle.

She said, "Part of me wants to call the funeral home and tell them they have to swap these for Mike, but for one thing, I'm scared they'll tell me he's already been scattered by the person who should have gotten these."

She finished her martini.

I said, "I really don't think that would be a good idea."

"I know it wouldn't," she said. "The person in that fishbowl was murdered."

She paused, almost as if she were listening to what she'd just said, hearing it for the first time. Then she started fixing herself another drink.

"Want one?" she said.

"No, thank you."

Then she sobered up so fast I wondered if she'd really been drunk, and she looked me right in the eye and said, "Why did you come here?"

I didn't know where to start. I didn't have time to explain everything to her, the whole year. So I jumped to the end. I said, "To tell you to be careful. I think your husband was murdered."

She didn't flinch.

I said, "I think mine was, too, and I think my mother was."

I didn't know which would be worse for her, being afraid of my father killing her when he probably wouldn't since for one thing, he had to stop somewhere, or not knowing that there was a chance she was in danger. I wasn't sure she would have been able to protect herself either way, from her own fears or from my father.

She said, "It's a serial killer?"

"No."

She poured some vodka in her glass.

"What, then?"

I couldn't say it. I took a deep breath.

I said, "My father."

I sat down and covered my face. I closed my eyes and looked at the darkness there inside me.

She didn't respond at all. She didn't move.

After a few minutes of silence, I said, "Mrs. Fontenot? Are you okay?"

She sort of smiled. She opened a drawer, took out some fish food, and walked over to her mantel. She dropped two pellets into the first bowl, and the fish started eating. "You know," she said, "it's funny, that I didn't think of that." She moved to the next bowl and put two pellets in it. "I knew about your mother, of course, and I saw that dreadful tape." She fed the third fish. "And then I knew enough to know I didn't want to know anything else." She fed the fourth one. "When Michael died, I did think it was odd, that he'd make that kind of mistake. He was always so careful with his guns." She fed the fifth one. "And later," she said, "I thought getting back the wrong bullet was odd, too, more than odd, but I never once put it all together." She fed the last fish. "I don't know why I didn't do that," she said.

I was afraid she was going to put food in her husband's bowl, but she didn't. She just set the canister of food next to it.

She took her glass and the bottle of vodka to her sofa and sat down.

I'd done all I could do for her, and I wanted to get out of there.

I said, "Today's the one-year anniversary of my mother's death."

"Has it already been a year?" she said.

"Well, it's three weeks earlier this year, but it was Mardi Gras. She died Mardi Gras night." Mardi Gras shifts with the church calendar.

"They say the first year's the hardest," she said.

"Yeah."

"And now, just when you get there, this with your husband."

She was shaking her head.

"Anyway, I need to be going."

I wanted to be in New Orleans for my mother. I wanted to go to the Cathedral and light the candle for her that I hadn't lit the night she died. Plus, I thought I'd be safe there, in the crowd. I didn't feel safe where I was.

I said, "Mrs. Fontenot?"

I was going to say goodbye. I was going to tell her to be careful, to get out of town, to keep quiet.

She looked up, almost surprised to see me still there.

She said, "You know, I've been thinking."

She stopped.

I said, "Yes?"

She said, "I think you're a more or less innocent party here, so I'm going to give you some advice from an old woman."

"Okay."

"Maybe you understand what kind of people you're dealing with and maybe you don't, but I suggest you learn how to exit a room."

Once, when I was twelve, Audrey told me, "Always enter a room while pretending that God is pulling a string from your vagina to the top of your head. And squeeze an imaginary doubloon between your buttocks."

I thought Mrs. Fontenot was losing it. I said, "Thank you for the advice."

Something was squeezing tight inside of me. Something felt like a pulling.

Mrs. Fontenot said, "Do you understand me?"

I said, honestly, "I'm not sure I do."

"Honey, learn how to know when to get up and walk out so you don't see or hear anything you'd be better off not knowing."

"Oh, I'm sorry. Of course, I'm sorry. And you're right. I'm just going now."

I reached in my purse for my keys, felt the gun there.

She drank her vodka straight, then poured herself another. She spoke almost as if she were talking to herself: "Whoever released that video knows too much for her own good and should start watching her back."

I felt something shattering inside me, something frangible.

I said, "Could I take you up on that cigarette offer now?"

She slid the pack across the coffee table.

My fingers were trembling. I took one and dropped it and picked it up off the floor. I was scared.

She poured herself another drink.

I said, "I'll just let myself out."

She drank it down and looked away.

On my way to the door, I grabbed the bullet fragments. On my way to the car, I dusted off the ashes.

So I LEAVE A MESSAGE FOR MY FATHER: *I have to talk to you. Meet me as soon as you can in Jackson Square. I'll be sitting on the steps in front of the Cathedral.*

And I go there, and I wait.

A group of drag queens walks past, all dressed as U.S. First Ladies—Jackie Kennedy, Barbara Bush, Martha Washington, some others it's harder to identify. A couple dressed as beer cans. An angel. A fat man wearing nothing but an alligator G-string wanders by with a woman in a housedress who could be his mother. And ordinary people wearing ordinary clothes.

After several hours—I don't know how many—a man walks through the crowd toward me. He's wearing a dark suit and a rubber mask, a Richard Nixon mask, of all things.

He sits down next to me and says, "Been here long?" It's my father's voice.

I'm halfway expecting him to kiss me on the cheek through the rubber, but of course he doesn't. He doesn't touch me. He barely looks at me.

I say, "Not too long."

Then I say, "Why Nixon?"

"It was lying around the house from last year's Christmas party skit. I didn't want to be recognized or filmed at Mardi Gras on the day of Carter's funeral."

Whatever.

I light a cigarette. I light it because I want it, I want to feel the way a cigarette makes me feel, and because I know he won't want me to. It's adolescent, but I don't know how else to say what I need to say to him, how to get him to hear me. If I told him he couldn't tell me what to do or how to live, he'd say something like, *And I wouldn't want to.*

He acts like he doesn't notice the cigarette, and I let out a long breath.

I say, "You didn't bring your security guards?"

"No."

"Are you wearing your bullet-proof vest?"

"Yes."

A vampire walks past us. A man with a Styrofoam headstone on his back throws up.

"Somebody wants you dead," I say. I'm not sure if it's a question or a statement.

He says, "It's just a precaution."

Now who's being paranoid?

We sit for what seems like a very long time without saying anything. The preacher is still going at it, though she's starting to lose her voice. If she gets her way, we're all going straight to hell.

I finish my cigarette. I grind out the ashes under my foot.

My father says, "What do you want, Grayson?"

"Would you take that ridiculous mask off?"

He pulls at it, rolls Nixon's skin off his face and tosses it aside.

"It's hot as hell in there," he says.

I say, "I guess so," and I smile.

We both know too many Nixon-in-hell jokes. Carter loved to tell Nixon jokes. That's a side of him I haven't been remembering. I haven't done him justice.

Now I'm trying not to cry.

He puts on a pair of dark glasses.

He says, "Tell me what you want."

I'm thirsty, and a man is selling drinks out of a giant fiberglass hot dog nearby, and I don't know if my father's offering me a drink or a bribe to keep my mouth shut or just asking me what I brought him here for, but I know what I want: I want him to die. I wish my own father were dead. I hate him that much—I hate him for all the time I spent, wasted, trying to love him and for everything he did to everybody else I loved, and I hate myself for hating him. I hate myself so much I wish he'd kill me.

I shake my head, as if I have no idea what I want.

He says, "I came here to apologize."

Please.

He says, "I wasn't there for you when your mother died. I wasn't there for you the night Carter died. I wasn't there for you most of your life. It's one of my greatest regrets. But I'd like to be here for you now."

Please God.

"If you need anything," he says. "If there's anything I can do."

It's the classic legal strategy—get away with murder by pleading guilty to a lesser offense. If his big crime in life was having been unavailable to me, I could forgive him, and I would. But if I tell him I forgive him for that, he'll apply my forgiveness to everything else he's done without ever having had to admit it, any of it, or be sorry for it or pay for it, and though he'll probably never admit or pay for anything anyway, I'm not going to be the one to absolve him.

I touch my hand to my lips. I press it there, partly to keep from trembling, partly to keep from saying anything because I'm afraid if I open my mouth, I'll start screaming at the top of my lungs.

Then I try to light another cigarette, but my fingers are limp, and I can't get the lighter to work. My father takes it out of my hands and lights it for me. I'm trying to work up the courage to tell him to fuck off, and I think he knows that, he's making it harder for me on purpose with his little gesture of civility. What I end up saying is, "Thanks." I take the cigarette.

He takes another and lights it for himself.

He says, "Maybe it's too late. Maybe there's nothing I can do. So if you can't forgive me, I'll understand. You don't have to explain. You don't even have to say another word. You can banish me from your life and choose never to see me or speak to me again—don't come to my funeral when I die—and I'll understand."

He's making me an offer: I can either buy into his half-baked apology, or he's out of my life forever. It's my choice. But there's no compromise. If I don't forgive him, if I don't let him get away with murder, and if I don't do it now, he won't give me another chance.

The doors to the Cathedral behind us open, and I turn to see the priest step back inside. He's ready to hear confessions, but nobody goes in.

I say, "That's not what I'm asking for."

"Then we're back to my original question," he says, with just a hint of businesslike impatience in his voice. He wants to finish this little negotiation. Get to yes. He says, "What do you want?"

I take a long drag on my cigarette. I'm trying to gather something inside me. Then I say, "The only way I can explain to myself why I married Carter in the first place, why I was so blind to how he was using me, what a jerk he could be, is that he told me he loved me, and in every other way, I thought he was just like you, so being loved by him felt like being loved by you."

Mardi Gras is circling around us, but I'm barely aware of it. I'm very focused, but I'm focusing on what's not happening instead of what is. He's not telling me he loves me. He's supposed to tell me he loves me, but he can't because he doesn't.

I say, "That sounds twisted. I didn't mean it that way."

Fuck.

He's not saying a fucking word.

I say, "But he wasn't like you. He tried, but he didn't come close. Because you're like God. You dispatch people like Carter, the people who believe in you, to destroy anybody you see as an enemy, and somehow, you convince yourself that your victims brought it on themselves."

"That's ludicrous," he says. He puts out his cigarette.

"Don't you mean blasphemous? See? You like the Old Testament God—and I've spent my life believing in both of you, but I don't anymore. I can't."

"I did not say blasphemous. It's ridiculous."

"You both hide in the shadows, running the world, and everybody's just supposed to say how great you are no matter what shit goes on down here. But meanwhile, anybody who dares to see your real face, dies. And now I see you, I see who you really are, and I feel like I'm dying. A part of me is dying, but it's the part that believed in you."

He lights a cigarette, one of mine, and smokes it. He smokes the whole thing while I wait, then crushes it under his foot.

He says, "Let's take a walk."

I stand up, and we move into the crowd. It's loud out here, too loud to talk. I don't know how much he heard of what I just said.

I'm trying to make myself pay attention, to see what's happening right in front of my face without trying to rewrite it in my head: He heard what I said. He's just not responding. Or he is responding, by walking away.

We're walking side by side in the direction of Canal Street, not saying a word.

I don't know where we're going, but traffic is blocked off in most of the Quarter, so I know I'm not in danger of being thrown into a car and carried away to an asylum as long as we stay on this side of Canal.

The Rex parade, the last one of Mardi Gras, is on its way from the Garden District, and the whole Quarter is building to a surreal frenzy. Even everyday activities like walking down the street feel charged with a tension like sexual energy. We pass a woman with an arrow that seems to go through her chest and a man wearing nothing but diapers and wings and carrying a bow, and they're sitting on a bench eating hot dogs with a topless woman whose head is in a toaster oven, her face looking out through the open door, her nipples tattooed with barbed wire. People are walking around in leather and chains and lingerie, exposing themselves, completely exposed. We pass a walking corpse and a man, asleep or unconscious, lying in an alley with his legs extending into the street, and we veer around him while the couple next to us steps over him. Nothing seems true.

A person could kill you, and it would take until tomorrow for anybody to realize you were dead. He could shoot you, and if he had a silencer on his gun, nobody would even turn their head to watch you fall down.

The closer we get to Canal, the louder and thicker the crowd gets, and the harder it is to navigate through them. They're waiting for the parade, building in layers toward mass hysteria.

I don't ask my father where we're going. I tell myself he wouldn't hear me if I did. I almost want to take his hand, in case we get separated, but I don't. I'm following him now instead of walking at his side, and I don't take my eyes off him.

When we cross Canal and go out of the Quarter, the atmosphere shifts almost immediately—it's quieter, calmer, easier to breathe— and for one brief moment I let myself think my anxiety was external, the crowds and the smells and the constant motion, the noise. But we keep walking through the Central Business District, and a car rolls toward us.

I think, This is it, I'm being kidnapped, they'll drug me and take me to an asylum.

I start walking faster. The car rolls past without even slowing down.

Nobody's trying to kidnap me. Even when I thought they were, I knew it wasn't a rational fear.

We keep walking without saying a word until we get to the Fairmont Hotel, where my mother died, and by the time we go inside, I'm roiling again.

We go into the Sazerac bar, where we drank with Carter's parents while my mother lay dying. A man in a tuxedo plays the piano, and we sit down together on a plush velvet sofa under the Huey Long mural. My father orders two Sazeracs.

I'm not going to say anything else until he responds to what I said in Jackson Square—how much more should I have to say?—though he seems just as determined not to say anything to me until I change the subject. It's a power game we're playing, though it's not a game and it's not play. It's also the way he told us to handle questions about his finances and romances and other unpleasant subjects during the campaign: whatever you say, say nothing.

When our drinks come, we each take a long swallow. My father orders another round, and the waiter nods and leaves.

I give up.

"Where's Audrey?" I say.

"With Carter's parents."

I finish my drink. I feel it rushing through me like fire, and I feel something between my father and me burning itself out, coming to an end. I feel it the way I felt both my marriages ending, with a mixture of resignation and terror and helplessness and relief. Whatever I say now may be the last thing I ever say to him, and I don't want to live the rest of my life with the same regrets for what was left unsaid that I have about my last conversations with Ray and with Carter. I want to be eloquent and articulate and brief but thorough.

But when I open my mouth to speak, all that comes out is, "You killed her."

My father smiles and nods at a couple across the room. Nothing's wrong, he's saying.

I try again: "I know you killed my mother and Carter and Dr. Fontenot."

Nothing. I get nothing from him.

The waiter brings the second round. I shouldn't drink any more right now, but I take a long swallow. My father hasn't finished his first one.

I pull Dr. Fontenot's bullet fragments out of my pocket and show them to him. They're sitting together like a wound in the center of the palm of my hand.

He barely glances at them.

It's possible he doesn't know what they are.

Then he puts his hand inside his jacket as if he's reaching for a gun, and I think, *This is it. Now he'll kill me.*

I take a deep breath. I'm ready.

But he gets out his wallet. He puts a fifty on the table for the drinks—he has a system of justice worked out in his head where if you overpay for some things, you don't have to pay for other things at all.

He says, "Here is not the place for this conversation." He stands up.

I follow him out of the bar and across the lobby of the hotel, and we get in the elevator together. He doesn't look at me, just like Carter, Carter in the elevator the night my mother died.

We're alone, but we don't speak. There's nothing left to say.

A crazy hope goes through me that a state trooper will be in his room, waiting, when we get there, and he'll handcuff my father, saying, "You have the right to remain silent," which strikes me in this mood as a line of poetry. The right to be quiet, to listen to silence and not be haunted by what you hear, to be safe. It's what I want for myself.

I touch my face.

I know my father won't be arrested, and I don't really think he'll kill me. I've heard of husbands killing wives, wives killing husbands, sons killing fathers, and brothers killing brothers, but I can't think of a time in history or legend or the news where a father killed his daughter. Plus, if he were going to have me killed, he would have done it before now, when there's nobody left to pin the blame on, so I'm trying to anticipate where this is going. If it were my mother in my shoes, telling me she knew he wouldn't kill her, I'd be afraid. I'd tell her, I hope you're right, but you should be prepared for anything.

Don't even go in the room with him, you should never have gone into the hotel. Run.

But I can't do it. I can't for the same reasons my mother couldn't. As much as I hate my father, I also love him desperately. I would give my life for him. In a way, I have given up several years of my life for him, which strikes me now as a waste, a wasted sacrifice, a wasted life.

Jesus Christ.

I'm not exactly cussing, but not really praying either. I'm thinking about God, wondering if he knows or cares where I am.

But by the time we get to my father's floor and the elevator doors slide open, I'm scared.

If there was a state trooper in here and he was waiting for anybody, he'd be waiting for me, waiting to take me to some mental hospital where my father could drug me and warehouse me and control me from a distance.

We walk down the hall and into the room, still without speaking. My father goes to the window and turns to face me.

I follow him in, past the bathroom, and stop. A light shines in from the bathroom door, which is just barely open.

But there's nobody in there, no cops. It's just my father and me and a light in another room.

His tuxedo is laid out on the bed for the ball like a dead body.

I lean against the wall farthest from him. I'm still holding Dr. Fontenot's bullet fragments in my hand, and I touch the wallpaper with the back of my fist.

"First," he says. "Before you walk off accusing people of murder, you should get your facts straight."His voice is smoky, almost hoarse.

I open my hand, and what's left of the bullet that killed Dr. Fontenot falls through my fingers and lands on the carpet without making a sound.

"I've spent the last nine months getting my facts straight," I say. "And I can't prove everything—I can't prove you killed Carter and Dr. Fontenot—but I can prove enough that you won't get away with killing my mother."

Then it's silent. My words hang in the air like unanswered prayers: You don't accuse my father of anything. If you do, you get fired, but he can't fire me.

Or killed. If you don't get fired, you get killed.

Part of me is waiting for him to kill me. Another part is waiting to go on with the conversation like normal people. But normal people, I realize, don't sit around accusing each other of triple homicide.

"Listen to me," he says. He speaks with slightly exaggerated enunciation, a thin layer of patience not meant to hide the rage beneath its surface. "I didn't kill your mother, and you damn well know it. I didn't kill Mike Fontenot, and I sure as fuck didn't kill Carter, who I loved like the son I never had. I don't blame you for what he did, but don't you dare go blaming me." He shakes his head. "Anybody else on this planet accuses me of murder, I would cut them off at the knees, mental illness or not."

He stops. Then he softens his voice. "But you're my daughter. So I'm going to get you some help. I love you."

I cover my face with my hands.

There it is, what I wanted: My father says he loves me. Or it's what I thought I wanted. It sits in my mouth like an aftertaste.

Something is over. But something else has just begun.

I'm trying to keep up.

When I open my eyes, he's not looking at me, he's looking toward the bathroom, and I turn to see what he's seeing: Audrey. She's standing in the bathroom doorway, leaning against the frame. She's wearing a white hotel bathrobe, but her hair is dry. She wasn't in the shower.

She's not moving, not saying a word. The expression on her face is blank. Whatever she knows, whatever she thinks, she wants at least one of us not to know what it is.

I turn to him, and he smiles at her, though he's not happy to see her.

Nothing's wrong, he's saying to her. Despite what you just heard.

He nods: *There's nothing Grayson can say that you can't hear. You know what her problem is. We'll just get her the help we both know she needs.*

He says, "How are Carter's parents?" and what he's asking is, *Are we in agreement here?*

She says, "Fine," her voice almost a whisper: *Yes, I am still with you. Though just barely.*

He goes to the armoire that holds the bar and opens it. He pours himself a drink.

He says to her, "Would you like anything?"

Do you need any more proof that she's crazy?

She says, "No. Thank you."

Case closed.

She's still not moving, not coming any closer to him. She's just standing there on the threshold, watching my father and me.

"Grayson?" He offers me a glass.

And something opens up in front of me or inside me—the world changes its shape, my soul does—and I say, "Make me a Sazerac," and he says he doesn't have the ingredients here and I say, "Then improvise," and I go to him and grab the glass and I'm thinking there aren't two kinds of bitters, there are thousands, and I pour whatever he was drinking into the bottom and say, "First, you spin it." I throw it more than swirl it into the air so it falls against the far wall and shatters to the floor.

My father stands where he is without moving.

He says, "That was unnecessary." He says it to me, his voice full of scorn.

I'm aching all over now. It's the weight of rage, and I'm not strong enough to keep holding it up. I sit on the end of the bed by the empty tuxedo.

"You don't love me." I whisper it, using all the strength I've got left just to form the syllables on my lips.

I stop. I let go of my purse, let it lie by my side on the bed.

He pauses, then shakes his head, almost sadly, and says, "This is not how I wanted this to go."

Something surges through me—his anger, or mine—and I say, "What, you wanted me to buy into your lies one more time? You expected me to believe I was safe with you when everybody else who touches you ends up dead?"

He's not answering me.

Audrey's not saying a word.

I'm getting louder. "How did you want it to go?"

He stands there in front of me, sipping his drink. Then he turns his back to me, walks to the desk. He doesn't hear me, doesn't see me, wishes I didn't exist.

I say, "I'm the one who released the tape."

He says, "You?"

He sets his glass down hard on the desk.

He heard me.

Audrey says, "Oh my God," and I turn to look at her, look in her eyes, and she meets my gaze. Then she covers her mouth with her hand.

I say to him, "She left it in my apartment, and I found it when I moved."

He turns to me, looks at me hard, shakes his head.

He says, "Why didn't you come to me?"

"Because of this," I say. "Because I was trying to avoid this exact, pathetic scene, where I tell you I know the truth, and you tell me I'm crazy."

He says, "Do you have any idea what you're responsible for?"

"Me? I'm responsible for this? *That* is crazy. *That* is insane. Try using that as a defense when you go on trial, that it's all my fault for turning you in, because that's what I'm going to do. I'll turn you both in if I have to."

Pick a side, Audrey. Now.

Her fingers still cover her mouth.

He laughs.

"You're good, Grayson," he says. He straightens his tie. "Now I'm not just a serial killer, I'm also insane? Have I got that right?"

I can't answer him.

"Audrey?" he says.

She lowers her hand.

He says, "Any thoughts you'd like to add here?"

She presses her palm to her chest and just barely shakes her head.

"You halfway believe Grayson, don't you?"

She doesn't answer.

"You believe her."

Nothing.

"Answer me, Audrey."

Then, in a whisper, "Yes."

He stops, lets the sound of her voice fill the room, then empty it.

He aims his glare back at me. "Well, well, well. You're in top form, Grayson. You've got yourself and Audrey all worked up into the same state of paranoia about me that you used to create in your mother. I almost admire your skill. But you overlooked one thing: If what you're saying were true, if I'm a cold-blooded triple murderer about to be caught . . ."

Then he stops again. He nods, as if he's playing back the last few words in his head: *if I'm about to be caught*. Considering his options.

And he reaches inside his jacket and pulls out a gun. He looks at it in his hand. He just barely nods: *if I'm about to be caught*.

Then he points it at me, at my heart.

"If I were a cold-blooded triple murderer about to be caught, do you think for one second I would let the two of you walk out of here? You think I'd hesitate to kill you? No. What would a killer do? You tell me, Grayson, since you know so much about how killers think."

I can't find words. I open my purse.

"No? No advice?"

I stand up. I show him my gun.

"Well," he says. "That's impressive."

He's not afraid of me.

I aim it at him, aim it across the room.

"Let's see," he says, taking a step toward me, toward my gun. "Two pistols, two women. If I were a killer about to be caught, it'd be tempted to shoot Audrey first, put her out of her misery as soon as possible, then finish off with you, so you'd take the whole story, beginning to end, to your grave. But you've got your own gun, so your bullets would have to kill Audrey. That's it. Anybody as ruthless as you think I am would kill you first, then use your gun to kill Audrey, then put my gun in Audrey's dead hand. So you killed each other. What a sad story. Tragic, really. Not to mention clever. But that's a cold-blooded murderer for you."

He comes another step closer to me. He stands there, just out of my reach.

"So come on, Grayson," he says, "what are you going to do about it? You've got your weapon. You can stop me. If this was all some kind of sick game on your part, then now's the time to throw in your cards. But if you really believe I killed your mother and your husband and Mike fucking Fontenot for good measure, then stop me from killing you."

He holds up his hands.

"Go on," he says.

His gun is over his head, aimed at nothing.

He says, "Don't let me get away with it."

And he waits. He's waiting for me to kill him.

But I can't do it. I take a step back, away from him.

"I thought not," he says, and he lowers his hands.

We have both been caught in lies.

And he smiles. It's a sly smile I've seen before, one that says, *We will keep each other's secrets.*

I take aim at him. I aim at his heart with both my hands, but my arms won't stop trembling, I can't keep him in the sight, so I take a step closer and he takes a step closer and I cock it and aim it and he comes at me fast and I fire but he's pushing me, pushing my arms, and I miss.

And for one tiny fraction of time, I have fired and I missed and that's all that has happened. We look at each other to go on from here, where he knows I would kill him, knows that I could, and I know he has to kill me.

But then Audrey lets out a breath and she falls toward the wall, she's falling and sliding, the wall rises up where she lies on the floor.

And my blood rises up in me, "Audrey," I'm screaming, he turns to me fast without watching her fall, and he touches my arm, he's not pushing or pulling, just touching me, making me choose what I do, and I look in his eyes and they're blank, without love, without fear— he still thinks he knows what I'll choose—and his gun is still locked in his hand and he hasn't aimed yet but he will, and he tightens his grip on my arm, but when I step back, he lets go, and my gun rises up toward his heart, toward his head, and it's aimed at his thought, and it fires.

And he throws back his head like he got the last laugh, but then he keeps going, his whole body falls back without catching itself and his knees don't collapse until it's too late. He falls on the floor and lands hard, so hard I can feel it, a thud, in my feet.

I stand and I look and I wait and he's fallen.

His eyes are still open, still blank, and the wound lies like ash on his forehead.

I put down my gun.

I go to his side and I kneel. I'm touching his face with my trembling fingers.

He's still warm.

He's dead.

I touch my father's fingers to my face, press them there.

Then I lay his hands at his sides. I close his eyes with my thumbs.

I close my own eyes, and I'm waiting, though I have no idea for what.

And then, "Grayson." It's Audrey.

"My God, you're alive!" and I turn to her, scramble across the floor to her side.

"In this kind of pain, I better not be dead," she says.

I smile through my tears. "Are you okay?"

"No," she says. "I've been shot."

"I'm sorry."

She's sitting up now, trying to move.

I say, "Stay where you are. I'll call for help."

But she crawls to my father, crawls to the spot where I stood when I shot him.

"Now give me your gun."

And I do what she says. I grab my gun and put it in her hand and sit down beside her. I want her to kill me. I deserve it.

She closes her fingers around the grip.

"Now dial nine-one-one," she says, "and give me the phone."

I do and she tells them her room number. "Come fast," she says. She looks in my eyes and says very slowly, "My husband has shot me."

She hands me the phone.

"Now go," she says.

"No."

"I'm going to tell them it was self-defense. Because it was."

"I'm not leaving you," I tell her. "I can't let you do this for me." She's bleeding, gasping for air.

"Then let me do it for my sister," she says.

I don't move. I can't.

"Get out, Grayson," through her teeth. "I'm not dying, but if this were my dying wish, that is what I would ask you."

I stay with her, holding her hand, until I hear the ambulance arrive. Then I prop open the door and slip into the service elevator, out of the hotel into darkness.

MIDNIGHT FINDS ME ON BOURBON STREET, where a group of cops walks slowly down Bourbon from Canal backed by two rows of mounted police. "Carnival's over," they yell as they move. "Clear the street." And the people crowd onto the sidewalks and begin to disappear into their hotels, leaving the street so bare so quickly that the wishful thought passes through my head that it didn't happen, none of it did. It was all an illusion.

"It's over," they say, and I'm watching the procession advance slowly, never varying their pace, and I'm watching Fat Tuesday succumb to Ash Wednesday, and it's like watching seconds move through time, night move into morning.

It's over.

When they get to the block where I'm standing, I slip down an alley and walk back to the hotel.

Laura hugs me tight when I walk in the room. They've been paging me for hours, she says. Then she sits me down and holds my hand and tells me she has bad news. My father's been shot, fatally. Audrey was also shot, but she was able to call 911. She's been taken off for surgery. The bullet punctured her lung but missed her heart, so she's expected to make a full recovery.

She doesn't know I know.

She doesn't want to know.

The cops are still there, just sitting around.

My father received a death threat yesterday afternoon, Laura tells me, so between that and Carter and Dr. Fontenot, he and Audrey were on edge. When my father walked in the hotel room, Audrey woke up and called out his name. She didn't hear him answer. People were partying in the hall. So she pulled out the gun and shot him, thinking he was an intruder, an assassin. Then, in the dark, he shot her back, apparently thinking she was. All a terrible accident.

They've taken my father to the morgue. Tomorrow, he will be cremated.

Laura says, "Are you okay?"

I'm shaking now, and crying.

I say, "I have to tell you something."

She puts her arms around me and strokes the center of my back and says, "Shh."

"But . . ."

"Shh."

And I stop. I sit up, out of her embrace.

She looks me in the eye.

"You have to be strong," she says.

Tomorrow morning, she says, she will take the oath of office as the new Governor of Louisiana.

While my father's body burns.

In a few days, we will seal his ashes up in a vault.

Laura promises me she'll be here for me.

"It's the best I can do," she says.

Then she says, "I'm sorry."

She asks me if I'd be willing to issue a public statement saying I know as well as anybody how living constantly under a death threat can lead to errors in judgment, mistakes that can and must be forgiven, and I hope the public will offer Audrey and me the kind of support and understanding we'll be giving each other during the difficult months to come.

I say, "I can do that."

She says, "Any questions?"

At least a thousand.

I say, "Not that I really want to hear the answers to right now."

I know the truth about my mother's death now—or most of it, which is all I thought I wanted. And maybe, in time, I will heal from its wounds. I'll find a way to sweeten part of what's bitter. I will fear no evil.

So I sit once again on the steps outside St. Louis Cathedral and wait here, quietly, for daylight. When it comes, I will go into the Cathedral, into the presence of God, or of Mystery, and a man who believes what he's saying will tell me what he knows of truth. Then he will lay his hand on my forehead and leave a tiny smudge of ashes in the center of it, a reminder of those truths in this life that remain unknowable, and I will open myself to mysteries greater than death and to the possibility of believing in them again.

I won't light a candle for my father.

I won't try to pray.

I will be still, though. I will listen to silence and know that I'm safe. And when I go, I will go in peace.